This Means War!

a Donovan Creed Novel - Volume 12
John Locke

TELEMACHUS PRESS

This book is a work of fiction. Names, characters, places and incidents are either the product of the author's imagination or are used fictitiously. Any resemblance to actual persons, living or dead, or to actual events or locales is entirely coincidental.

THIS MEANS WAR!

The publisher does not have any control over and does not assume any responsibility for author or third-party websites or their content.

Cover Designed by: Telemachus Press, LLC
Copyright © Shutterstock/152214749

Visit the author's website:
http://www.donovancreed.com

Published by: Telemachus Press, LLC
http://www.telemachuspress.com

ISBN: 978-1-941536-73-5 (eBook)
ISBN: 978-1-941536-74-2 (Paperback)

Version 2014.12.01

Printed in the United States of America

10 9 8 7 6 5 4 3 2 1

To Jed Barish of Las Vegas, Nevada.
Cat rescuer, businessman, and doer of good deeds
whenever possible.

This Means War!

PART ONE:
Sadie Sharp

Who's Sadie Sharp, and why should we care?

SADIE, AGE 24, IS an amazing young lady who suffers from a unique form of ASD (Autism Spectrum Disorder) that makes it difficult for her to relate to others. She's incapable of feeling—or understanding—positive human emotions such as empathy, humor, gratitude, and love. Conversely, she *is* able to feel anxiety, dread, fear, and possesses a skill set crucial to survival, including adaptability, a heightened sense of awareness, and courage.

Sadie's a survivor.

She's extremely task-oriented, fair-minded, and has overcome incredible obstacles to create a life that's generally normal. For example, she can drive. Shop. Attend classes. Communicate. Function at a high level when exposed to routines, such as waking up at the same time each morning to the scent of fresh coffee brewing in the pre-set coffee machine, brushing her teeth, peeing, then walking down the hallway from her bathroom to the kitchen as she's doing right now.

Sadie's married.

Does her best to socialize with neighbors Carol and Kenny, and husband Rick's friends, all of whom know better than to play tricks or head games...

...Which is why she's going to be very confused, upset, and disoriented two seconds from now when she turns the corner and sees the note on the kitchen counter, by her car keys.

Three-words, lettered in script:

Tonight you die!

Chapter 1

SADIE GRABS HER cell phone, calls her husband.

"What's wrong?" he asks.

"Tonight you *die*? *Seriously*, Rick?"

He pauses a moment. "Are you off your meds?"

Sadie fights the urge to curse him, takes a deep breath before saying, "I woke up, went to pour a cup of coffee, saw my keys on the counter."

"So?"

"I never leave my keys on the kitchen counter."

Rick sighs. "I have no idea what you want me to say."

"I want you to admit you put my keys on the counter and wrote this stupid note. And I want to know why."

"Sadie, listen to me. This whole conversation's crazy! I never touched your car keys. I didn't write you a note."

The tone of his denial is so convincing it takes a moment before the reality sinks in. When it does, it hits them hard.

Someone's been in their house! He–or they–could still be here!
Rick speaks first: *"Jesus,* Sadie! *Run!"*

Chapter 2

SADIE GRABS HER car keys.

Rick shouts, "Get out of the house! Run to the car! *Now!*"

"I'm not dressed."

"*What? Are you insane? Run!*"

She *is* dressed, if she's being technical: scoop-neck t-shirt, panties, slippers. It's just that she's not dressed appropriately for running terror-stricken through the neighborhood. Not that Rick said to run through the neighborhood in her underwear. He said get in the car and drive away. Okay, simple enough. Sadie's already got the keys in hand.

She rushes to the door that leads to the garage, but stops short. Thinking: *I never leave my keys on the kitchen counter.*

Which means whoever's after her *expects* her to enter the garage. He strategically placed the keys for that very purpose. He *wanted* her to scoop them up and run to her car. It's the obvious thing to do. Even Rick said it just now.

"Sadie?" he says. "What's happening? Are you in the car yet?"

"No."

"Please hurry! And let me know when you're safe."

"The keys," she says.

"What about them?"

"You honestly didn't put them on the counter this morning?"

"No, of course not."

"Neither did I."

"So?"

"Think about it."

He does. "Shit, you're right. Stay out of the garage! Go out the back door and run to Carol's."

"But—"

"You're not safe at home, Sadie! Run to Carol's."

"You're *scaring* me!"

"You *need* to be scared. *Listen:* I'm giving you a *task*. Get out of the house. Run to Carol's. Tell her to lock her doors and get her gun."

"You'll meet me at Carol's?"

"Yes. I'm leaving the office right now. I'm calling 911."

"Okay. Hurry!"

"I'm on my way."

Sadie hangs up, races out the back door, sprints across the deck, but hears heavy footsteps coming up behind her. She screams, makes the split-second decision to vault the railing instead of negotiating the four steps that lead to the yard. It was a good idea, possibly a life-saving one, except that her trailing leg catches the top spindle and sends her plummeting face-first onto the grass. Sadie hits and rolls, looks up just in time to see....

Nothing.

There's no one there.

Had she really heard footsteps?

Absolutely. There's no doubt. Unless...

Unless they were the echo of her own footsteps.

Stupid! she thinks. She could have broken an ankle.

Sadie scrambles to a sitting position and darts her eyes around nervously, like a squirrel in a yard full of dogs.

Everything feels safe. Now that she thinks about it, even the house felt safe when she was on the phone with Rick. But the garage?

Not so safe.

The killer's in the garage. *Has* to be in the garage. She can *feel* it. He's in there now, possibly in the back seat of her car, waiting for her. Should she go back in the house and lock the door? Try to trap him there till the police show up?

No. She shakes her head at her stupidity. He's probably got a key to the house. And if not, he could still kick the door open and get her.

Rick's right. Safe thing is go to Carol's. And quickly.

So why's she sitting on her ass in the back yard?

Because she can't help wondering what the killer has planned for her. Will he attack her suddenly, like an urban looter after a police shooting? Or rape her methodically, over time, like a Senate reform bill? Will he force her in the trunk of her own car and drive to a secluded spot? Make her dig her own grave?

Sadie shakes the scary thoughts away and concentrates on what she knows: one, someone's trying to kill her. Two, she's got a short window of time to get to Carol's. Three, Carol's got a gun and knows how to use it.

She presses Carol's number on speed-dial and puts the phone on speaker. Then gets to her feet and starts running. Considers tossing out a scream for good measure, but fears attracting the killer's attention.

By the time Carol's phone goes to voice mail, Sadie's on the porch, banging on Carol's door. Gets no response, so she calls Carol's name. Gets nothing; turns, glances behind her.

Though Sadie sees and hears nothing, every hair on the back of her neck stands on end. Every synapse in her brain registers fear. Her instincts tell her a dangerous predator is within striking distance, and she's the prey.

One thing about neighbor Carol: she's always home. So why isn't she answering her phone or door? Is the killer *here*?

Sadie takes a deep breath, tries the door.

Surprisingly, it's unlocked.

With a great sense of foreboding, Sadie pushes it open a couple of inches and whispers, "Carol?"

There's a scent.

Not a stench, but a smell that's definitely out of place.

Fearing the worst, Sadie pushes the door completely open, takes a moment to focus...then shrieks.

It was a single shriek, more instinct than shock, as she had a general premonition of what to expect before opening the door. But what she sees: another note—calms her instantly and reminds her that the killer's first note said Sadie would die *tonight*, not this morning, which means if the killer can be trusted, Sadie's safe for the time being. She's also relieved to see neighbor Carol sitting in a chair, ten feet from the front door, grinning hideously, holding a gun.

Except that...Carol's dead.

The knife planted hilt-deep in Carol's chest removes any doubt as to cause of death, but the wide, bloody smile carved across her face, *Joker*-style, reveals the killer's sadistic streak.

The cardboard sign on Carol's chest, held firmly in place by the knife that killed her, reads:

You Are So Predictable!

Chapter 3

REALLY? SADIE THINKS. *I'm predictable? Wouldn't it have been predictable to grab the keys and run to the car?*

Rick thought so.

Is *he* predictable too?

And is it predictable to stand out here on Carol's porch, staring at her neighbor's body, debating how predictable she's been up to now?

Sadie thinks not.

And she doubts the killer could have predicted she'd only scream once, or that she's currently resisting the urge to flee the scene.

Why *isn't* she screaming and running from Carol's house?

Because those reactions would be highly predictable.

But you know what *wouldn't* be?

Entering Carol's house.

Sadie does so, closes the door behind her, locks it, and studies Carol's body carefully, wondering, *Why would someone want to kill me so badly they'd kill my neighbor just to frighten me?*

She gives Carol a stern look. "How did you let this *happen?* You had a *gun!*"

She walks to the powder room, locks herself inside, figuring it's as good a place as any to wait for Rick and the police.

Speaking of Rick....

She tries his cell phone.

No answer.

She'd like to turn on the faucet to wash her face, but can't take a chance on the noise.

Wait. *Noise?*

Sadie laughs at the notion the noise from the faucet could possibly matter after the commotion she made on the doorstep moments ago. If Carol's killer's in the house, he already knows where she is. She leans over the sink, turns on the faucet, washes her face. Then checks herself in the mirror and sees a message reflected on the wall behind her, written in blood:

Tonight you die!

Under normal circumstances Sadie would gasp, or even scream. But her current tasks are clear: wait for help, and remain unpredictable. She turns and focuses on the bloody message. Was it meant for *her,* or Carol?

Not Carol, she thinks. Because how could the killer expect Carol to see a message written on the wall of her powder room? It's not the bathroom Carol would use during the course of a normal day.

It's for guests.

The blood is almost certainly Carol's, which means the message was written after her attack, and almost certainly after her death. Believing otherwise would mean the killer brought someone else's blood to the scene, and that's not likely unless...

...Unless Carol's house is a killing field.

As Sadie tries to summon the courage to search Carol's house for bodies, her phone rings. Thinking it's Rick or the 911 operator, she puts it to her ear.

"Sadie?"

"Yes?"

"Tonight you die!"

Chapter 4

"WHY?" SADIE WANTS to yell, but the killer hangs up before she gets the word out.

She presses the redial button. After two rings, the killer answers, saying, "You finally surprised me, Sadie. What do you want?"

"I want to live."

"Don't we all?"

"I suppose. But most of us don't have to ask permission."

He pauses a moment. "Would you like an extra day?"

"You'd consider it?"

"I might. But you'd have to earn it."

"How?"

"By killing someone."

"*What?*"

"You want to live another day? Kill someone."

"Who? Rick?"

"What made you say Rick?"

"Uh...I'm not sure."

"You *want* to kill your husband?"

"No, of course not!"

"And yet his was the first name you thought to mention."

"I guess I figured if you know me, you must know Rick."

"And?"

"You'd realize how easy it would be to kill him."

"Why is that?"

"He'd never suspect it. Not from me, anyway. Plus..."

"Yes?"

"He trusts me."

The killer says, "I may have underestimated you."

"I get that a lot." She pauses a moment, then says, "Who would I have to kill?"

"Your choice," he says. "Surprise me. But do it before five p.m."

"I can't just kill some random person!"

"Then...tonight you die!"

A million thoughts flood Sadie's brain, all of them bad. "*Wait!*" she says.

"What now?"

"I'll do it."

"You're sure?"

"Uh huh."

"Say it."

"I'll kill someone. Today, before five p.m."

"You have someone in mind?"

"Are you *crazy?*"

"You want to rephrase that?"

"Sorry. I mean, no, I haven't thought it through yet. But I'll do it."

"Good to hear. By the way, you'd be smart to leave Carol's house before the police arrive."

"That makes sense. Can I ask you something?"

"Go ahead."

"Is this some sort of horrible joke?"

"Ask Carol."

"Good point."

They're both quiet till Sadie says, "Okay. I've got an idea."

"About what?"

"Who to kill."

"You mean whom."

"Whom?"

"If we're being grammatically precise you'd say *whom.*"

"I'm not good at grammatics."

"Grammatics?"

"Or whatever it's called," Sadie says. "Is it really that important?"

"It was to my father. Every time I violated a rule of grammar he broke one of my fingers." He waits for her to respond. When she doesn't, he says, "What, no sympathy?"

"What do you mean?"

"Most women would say, 'Oh, how awful!'"

"Why?"

"Because my father was a monster."

"Oh. Sorry. Uh...I'm not sure how to respond."

"Because?"

"I have difficulty expressing certain emotions."

"I actually know about your ASD. I was testing you to make sure I wasn't misinformed. Anyway, according to dear old dad, grammar's the difference between feeling you're nuts and feeling your nuts."

"Huh?"

The killer sighs. "Not important. Correcting people's grammar is a character flaw. It's kept me single these many years. Surprised?"

"That you're single? No. But I doubt grammar's been the stumbling block."

"We're getting sidetracked. You were about to reveal your victim."

"I don't know...*whom*...I'm going to kill yet, I just have a good idea where to find him. Or her."

"You almost sound enthusiastic."

"That's just me, having a task."

"Out of curiosity, where does a person such as yourself go to find a victim on such short notice?"

"You said I could surprise you."

He laughs. "Indeed I did."

"Then you'll have to wait and see."

"Fair enough. Sadie?"

"Yeah?"

"What's happened?"

"What do you mean?"

"A moment ago you were terrified. Screaming, running, carrying on. Now you're as calm as a tree shadow. It's incongruous."

"I don't see why. You gave me an extra day to live, and a task to focus on. I'm grateful, and about to be very busy."

"It's just a day, Sadie. And I seriously doubt you're capable of feeling gratitude for it."

"Maybe not, but I can certainly understand you've doubled my time left on earth."

"You know what I think? I think you're just playing along, hoping to buy time, expecting the police to protect you."

"Not true. I'm highly task-oriented. I'll get it done. I'll kill someone today. You'll see."

The killer laughs. Says, "Well, *this* should be interesting!"

Chapter 5

CONFIDENT THE KILLER is far removed from the general area, Sadie wastes no time leaving Carol's. Could he be waiting for her in the garage after all? Of course. But she'd bet against it. He seemed sincere on the phone just now, confiding how he's single and how his father mistreated him and all.

Not that Sadie gives a shit.

Lots of kids have been abused by their parents. But none of *them* killed Carol.

Only him.

She pauses. Only *he*?

She crosses her back yard to the deck, sees one of her slippers on the ground, realizes she just casually walked home from Carol's in her underwear, in a single slipper, like Cinderella. She picks it up and wonders if anyone saw her, and if so, will they call Rick and ask if she's off her meds again? She sighs, climbs the four steps to the deck; enters the house far calmer than she left it minutes ago—despite having spoken to the man who promised to kill her tonight. Or to-morrow night, assuming she completes her task.

Sadie checks her watch. On the surface, nine hours seems a generous amount of time to kill a total stranger. But there are a number of potential time-sucks. Chief among them, Rick and the police will be arriving any minute. It's either leave before they get here, or spend countless hours answering questions. But if she leaves, will they think the killer abducted her? Will they put out an alert? Contact the media? Set up roadblocks? Track her phone and credit cards?

She wonders anew why Rick hasn't called her back. And while she's on the subject, why haven't police or emergency personnel responded? Does it really take this long for 911 to dispatch a police car to the scene of a potential murder? It's not like Alexandria's a hick town in the middle of nowhere. It's a major city, just six miles south of D.C. And her house is within walking distance of Old Town, where boutiques, restaurants and antique stores generate more customers than Free Chicken Day at KFC. What she's thinking, someone should have been here by now.

She tries Rick again but gets no answer. A shame, really, since Rick would almost certainly be interested to know Carol's been stabbed to death. He's been fucking her for two months, after all.

Not that Sadie's supposed to know. That part's sup-posed to be a big secret. Even Kenny—Carol's husband—didn't know till Sadie told him a few weeks ago.

Kenny didn't take it well.

His face turned red, then purple, then contorted into an expression that looked like a clay ashtray molded by a second-grader.

Poor Kenny.

He screamed, "I'll kill them *both!*" but now someone's beaten him to it. Or at least beaten him to Carol.

Sadie enters her closet, dresses quickly as possible. Pees, brushes her teeth, checks her hair in the mirror.

She's twenty-four, great hair, nice face, decent body. Rick's friends call her Sexy Sadie—after the Beatles song—and rate her a solid eight on the ten-scale, which means she's pretty enough to turn heads and stimulate bone growth in oversexed males, but not so pretty they'd put up with her mental issues.

She wonders who told the killer about her ASD. It means he knows how she responds to specific tasks, and how she reacts to sensory aspects of her environment. It strikes her the killer could use this information to manipulate her behavior, and she'd be powerless to resist.

Though Carol's murder shocked and frightened Sadie, she won't mourn the loss of her friend. Won't miss her. Won't associate feelings of grief, guilt, or even concern for Carol's loved ones. Sadly, Carol's death won't amount to a blip on Sadie's radar now that her life has ended.

She'd love to have normal emotions. Can't imagine how it would feel to be jealous, hurt, or in love. Rick—in moments of anger—calls her a robot, and says she has less empathy than a used Tampon. She doesn't take it personally. In fact, she takes nothing personally.

She checks her phone. Still no word from Rick or the police.

In the kitchen now, she pauses. She can walk to the kill-ing place in fifteen minutes, or drive there in three. If she walks, they'll think she's been kidnapped. If she drives, someone might spot her car.

She decides to walk.

Her destination—Magic Manor Nursing Home—is the perfect place to commit a murder. It offers Sadie a wide vari-ety of old, sick people who are already at death's door. How bad could it be to slightly speed the process for one of them?

She exits her front door humming *My Brave Face*, as if not having a care in the world, but that façade crumbles the moment her feet hit the sidewalk. That's when paranoia kicks in, along with the overwhelming sense all eyes are on her, and total strangers are studying her every move. And why shouldn't they? There's a killer's on the loose. She picks up the pace and catches herself striding in lockstep to *Riders on the Storm*:

There's a killer on the road...

She finally arrives at Magic Manor, walks down the hall, enters Room 24, the same room she visits every week, pulls up a chair, and patiently listens to her mother's litany of complaints covering every mind-numbing aspect of nursing home life, from bingo to bedsores to next week's dessert menu. Sadie bides her time, waits for the inevitable gossip session. When her mom unloads, no resident is spared. But instead of tuning her out, Sadie listens to every word and learns there are three women on the brink of death: Evelyn Carstairs, Room 18; Myra Biggelo, Room 12; and Cecile O'Neal, right next door.

When her mom falls asleep, Sadie takes the pillow from the guest chair, checks the hall to make sure she's alone, then quietly creeps into Cecile's room.

Thankfully, Cecile is sleeping.

Sadie crosses the floor swiftly, thinking, *the faster I work the sooner I'll finish*. But as she approaches, Cecile's eyes open. She sees the pillow and says, "Are you here to kill me?"

Sadie's ASD makes it extremely difficult to lie. But if she answers truthfully, Cecile might scream or press the buzzer hanging from the handrail. Sadie takes a moment to calculate the likelihood of Cecile's old, arthritic claw of a hand reaching the button before Sadie can prevent her from pressing it. While she likes her chances, she takes a step closer to hedge her bet. Then says, "I heard the bad news. I'm so sorry."

Cecile says, "I was in the hospital two weeks before the doctors said there was nothing they could do. Then they sent me back here to die."

"Are you in pain?"

Cecile smiles a sad smile. "It's not so bad. My loneliness hurts worse than the cancer."

"I can end your suffering."

Cecile nods. "Did my granddaughter send you?"

"Excuse me?"

"My granddaughter could certainly do it, but she refuses to visit. Won't even call on my birthday, or Christmas."

"Are you sure about that? Because sometimes my mom forgets when I visit."

"There's nothing wrong with my memory, child. I always knew I'd end up this way. My name's an anagram, you know."

Sadie frowns. "Cecile is?" She thinks a moment, then shakes her head. "I'm usually good with puzzles, but you've stumped me. Unless there's a different way of spelling it."

"Not Cecile," she says. "O'Neal." She spells it.

Sadie smiles. "Got it! Last two letters go first. O'Neal is an anagram for *alone*."

Cecile smiles back. "You're a clever one."

"Thanks. Does anyone else visit you?"

"There *is* no one else. I only had one child. She got married, had a daughter of her own."

"Your daughter won't visit?"

"She's dead. Got killed by her *own* daughter, the one I mentioned."

Sadie cocks her head. "Your granddaughter murdered her *mother?*"

"Killed *both* her parents, if you want the truth. Killed 'em both and spared me to mourn 'em."

"Someone's trying to kill me, too," Sadie says, moving the pillow closer to Cecile's face.

Cecile looks at her with great curiosity. "Who, child?"

"I don't know. Some random guy called me on the phone. He killed my neighbor and says he's going to kill me, too."

"When?"

"Tomorrow."

"You should kill him first. That's what I'd a' done if I'd known the type a' kid we had in the house. I'd a' killed my granddaughter the minute she got attacked, raped, and left for dead."

Sadie tries to make her voice sound properly horrified: "Omigod! That's *terrible!*"

Cecile nods. "Gordon Day's the one who did it. But they never reported him."

"Why not?"

"Mr. Day owned the company my son-in-law worked for. He paid 'em plenty to keep their mouths shut. 'Course, that didn't set right with my granddaughter. When she got old enough she killed her parents. Killed Gordon Day, too, and some others, before they finally put her away."

"She went to prison?"

"Crazy house."

"I'm so *sorry!*" Sadie says, pleased with the amount of emphasis she put in her response. "But how could you expect her to visit if she's locked away?"

"She's out now. Been out for a half-dozen years."

Sadie looks at the pillow and says, "I should get this over with."

"Go ahead, child, I won't put up a fight. But this man who's threatening to kill you? You should kill him first."

"I wouldn't know how."

"Call my granddaughter. She'll know someone who can do it."

Sadie laughs. "I don't think so. Your granddaughter sounds awfully dangerous."

"More dangerous than the man who's going to kill you?"

"Good point."

"Call my granddaughter. It's what she does. For a living."

"She kills people?"

"For a price."

Sadie mulls it over. "Do you happen to know her phone number?"

PART TWO:
Ryan Decker

Who's Ryan Decker,
and why should we care?

DECKER'S A FORMER urban terrorist, currently working for Homeland Security.

He's also Donovan Creed's arch enemy.

Chapter 1

16 Hours Later...

RYAN DECKER, SITTING on a three-legged stool, makes the final adjustment to the hose. "You sure you want to be a part of this?"

"I wouldn't miss it for the world," his new girlfriend coos.

Decker looks her over in the bright lights he placed around the perimeter to give passersby the impression he's nothing more than a midnight water company employee, repairing a water line. She's young, pretty, and crazier than bees in a cyclone. He runs through his mental checklist, says, "Anyone approaches, I'll do the talking."

She, sitting on a picnic cooler, says, "You think it'll work?"

"Why wouldn't it?"

"Seems too easy."

"Five-sided wrench, two lengths of hose, pump, barrel of toxic chemicals, a rudimentary understanding of hydraulics...."

"It's the rudimentary part that makes me nervous," she says. "Has anyone done a formal study on this?"

"Actually, yes. The idea came from a report Donovan Creed sent to Homeland Security months ago. It's all theory, of course, since field testing would require poisoning a portion of the populace. But it's diabolically simple. I'm convinced it'll work."

"You're saying that common, everyday fire hydrants are so vulnerable to terrorist attacks that a single person can poison an entire neighborhood in the space of ten minutes?"

"That's what I'm saying."

"But hydrants are everywhere!"

"That's the point Creed was trying to make. He said there are more than 6 million fire hydrants in the country. More than 109,000 in New York City alone."

"Why haven't the water companies acted on the report?"

"Homeland hasn't shared it with them."

"Why not?"

"They have to weigh the likelihood of an attack against the likelihood of provoking one."

"Can you say that in my native language: English?"

Decker laughs. "Homeland got the report last February, so by now they've probably formed a secret committee to study what Creed calls NHP."

"What's that?"

"Neighborhood Hydrant Poisoning. But the government can't afford to reveal the problem until they have a viable solution ready to implement. Otherwise, the public will panic, and terrorists will start attacking hydrants like Don Quixote attacks windmills."

She shows him a skeptical look. "Walk me through it."

"You know how fire hydrants work, right?"

"Pretend I don't."

"Okay, so hydrants are connected to large underground pipes that carry water to homes, businesses, and schools."

"That much I knew."

"Good. Check this out." He opens the hydrant cover with the wrench to expose the opening and says, "This part works like the spigot above your sink or bathtub. After attaching the hose I can make the water flow at fifty to eighty psi, which is pounds per square inch."

He connects the hoses to the hydrant, the pump, and the drum filled with toxic chemicals.

She watches the progress a few seconds, then says, "I hate to burst your bubble, but all you're doing is forcing water into the chemical drum."

"For now," Decker says. "But see this other valve on the hydrant? When I open it and pump the pressure in the hose above eighty psi, it'll create a backflow."

"What's that mean?"

"It means I'll create a pressure imbalance in the barrel that'll force the chemical waste back through the hydrant into the water system. Within minutes the pipes and taps of the entire neighborhood will be filled with poison."

"But this is *your* neighborhood! The poison's going into *your* home."

"That's right."

"What about Jill?"

"What about her?"

"Does she *know*? Have you *warned* her?"

"No."

"She could die."

"It's a strong possibility."

She looks at him and smiles. "You like me more than her."

"I do."

"But we've only been together a week!"

"Two, if you count my time in the hole."

"Don't be vulgar."

"I meant—"

"Relax," she says. "I'm kidding. Wanna know what I think? I think you're poisoning your own neighborhood hoping the FBI will blame Creed. You think they *will*?"

"Possibly. Eventually."

"That's...um...what did you call it? Diabolical?"

He smiles. "You like that word."

"I do. I'm gonna say it a lot from now on." As she watches him work, she says, "I know why you're with me."

"Tell me."

"You want to push Creed's buttons."

Decker nods. "I won't deny it. That was the original plan. But now that we've spent fifty-plus hours in the sack?"

"Yeah?"

"I'm all yours."

Rachel Case smiles. "I'm told I'm good in bed."

"You are for a fact."

"Best you ever had?"

"By far! And I'm not just saying that. I can't believe Creed abandoned you!"

"Join the club," she says. "Can I be the one to turn on the pump?"

"You want to?"

She nods.

"Be my guest."

He opens the valve. Rachel says, "Now?"

He nods.

She starts the pump. "How long before people start dying?"

"I have no idea. But maybe you should go ahead and pour the champagne."

"Why?"

"In case it doesn't work."

"I don't want to celebrate if it doesn't work."

He checks the drum. "It'll work."

"How many innocent people will die?"

"Dozens, possibly hundreds."

"That is so *hot*! Are *we* in danger?"

"Only if the barrel blows up. In which case we die, and the neighborhood lives."

"Cool!"

Decker's phone rings. He clicks it on, listens a moment, then says, "Are you *serious?*" Then he says, "*Holy shit! Where?*"

Decker talks some more, then hangs up and says, "It's started."

"What has?"

"World War Three."

"What are you *talking* about?"

"Someone just detonated a nuclear weapon on American soil."

"*Who?*"

"Terrorists, I assume."

"Where?"

"Rural Virginia. They want us to go back to Area B, Mount Weather."

"*Us?*"

"They said I can bring someone. I'm choosing you."

"Forget it. I didn't spend the last two years trying to get out of that shithole just to go back."

He nods slowly. "I don't blame you."

"I trusted you to get me out," she says. "It's why I fucked you the first hour we met. It's why I'm with you now."

"I know."

"*Do* you Ryan? Because I would've fucked Charles Manson if he'd gotten me out first."

"I get it, Rachel. Don't worry, I won't make you go back."

"I don't want *you* going there, either."

"Why not?"

"I've grown fond of you."

"*Fond?*" He laughs. "What're you, eighty years old?"

He turns his attention to the chemical drum as it forces the toxic waste into the hydrant. "Well, it works," he says. "But...."

"Yeah, I know, baby. It's anti-something-or-other."

"Climactic?"

"Yeah. Like you planned to take a monster shit, but only farted."

He frowns. "Thanks for putting it in perspective for me."

"My pleasure. Wanna fuck?"

"You mean *now*? Right *here*? In the middle of all these lights?"

"Why not?"

He looks around. "I'm game if *you* are."

"Just so you know, I'm proud of you," she says.

"Why?"

"How many people can kill dozens to hundreds of innocent people in ten minutes without getting caught? It's a hell of an achievement!" She hands him a plastic cup of champagne, and holds hers up to offer a toast. They click plastic and scarf their drinks. Then she pulls her pants to her ankles and says, "Front or back?"

"Ladies' choice," he says.

"I guess I don't need road grease on my butt," she says. "How about doggy-style?"

Decker says nothing.

"Ryan?"

She looks at him closely, then shrugs and pulls her pants back up. Seeing his phone in his hand, she takes it, punches in a number. When Donovan Creed answers, she says, "Decker's dead."

"You're sure?"

She checks his pulse. "Yup. The poison worked. Your plan was...diabolical."

"Thanks."

"I'd thank you for helping me get released, but since you took your sweet time doing it, I'll just say fuck you."

"You think it was *easy* getting Decker to Area B? Figuring out a way to lure him into finding you without being obvious?"

"How'd you know he'd want me?"

"He was very competitive. I knew he'd want what I had."

"Say it."

"My former girlfriend."

"*Former?*"

Creed sighs. "We've been through this, Rachel."

"You're *dumping* me?"

"Yeah. Except this happened nearly two years ago, remember?"

"Whatever. So when do I get my money?"

"It's already in an account in your name. When you hang up I'll text you the information."

"Okay." She pauses. "I'd tell you to fuck off, but I need the money."

"I know."

She looks at Decker. Then says, "*Fuck!*"

"What's wrong?"

"This was a huge mistake. I never should have poisoned him. He would've taken good care of me."

"Sorry to break it to you, but he only wanted to fuck you and get whatever information he could out of you. Still, I'm surprised you went through with it."

"I almost didn't, but then he called me old."

"*Old?* When?"

"Just now. I told him I'd grown fond of him and he said, 'What're you, eighty years old?' I can't abide that."

"If it's any consolation, he needed to die. And he would've killed *you*, eventually."

"But now I don't have him *or* you. I'm completely, totally, hopelessly alone. What am I supposed to *do?*"

"It's ten million dollars, Rachel. You can do *anything.*"

"But I'm crazy. You know that, right?"

"I know a lot of crazy multi-millionaires. Trust me, no one will notice. They'll think you're eccentric."

"I know what I'll do!"

"What's that?"

"I'll go live with Jill."

"Decker's girlfriend?"

"*Former* girlfriend. I'm gonna go knock on her door and say, 'Whatever you do, don't drink the water!'"

"The water?"

"Yup."

"What's wrong with the water?"

"She'll be so grateful, she'll let me move in with her. Before you know it, we'll be best friends. It's diabolical!"

Creed pauses. "I'm not completely sure what you're talking about, but I expect friendships have been built on flimsier foundations. Good luck, Rachel. When you hang up

I'll text the banking information to the phone you just called me on."

"Okay. Bye."

PART THREE:
Mike & Jimmy

Who are Mike & Jimmy, and why should we care?

MIKE'S ON THE run. Jimmy's his friend.

It's not what you think: Mike's not a criminal; he's one of five living Americans who can identify the terrorist who detonated the nuclear bomb in Virginia three nights ago. He's also the only known survivor of the blast.

Mike fears the terrorist who got away, which is why he's seeking a place to hide. What he doesn't realize, lots of scary people are looking for him.

Including Donovan Creed.

Chapter 1

"JESUS, MIKE. YOU okay? You look like ten miles of bad road."

"Thanks."

"No, seriously, man. Who did that to you? Your face, your arms? Were you burned?"

"It's a long story."

"What're you doing in Houston? I thought you lived in...uh..."

"Charlottesville."

"Right. Are you visiting?"

"It's a long story."

"Wanna tell me over dinner? I could use a good salad."

"*Salad?*" Mike says. "Are you *shitting* me? *Fuck* the salad. It's bourbon and steak for us. Followed by more bourbon."

"You payin'?"

"Of course...if I can crash here a few days."

"Uh...I'll have to check with the missus on that—"

45

"Man rule number one," Mike says, "You don't *ask* your wife for shit, you *tell* her!"

Jimmy laughs. "No wonder you're divorced. Tell you what: we'll grab some dinner, I'll call Millie. She says no, I'll pick up the check."

"Deal."

"Saying that, I don't foresee a problem, other than cholesterol. You dead set on steak?"

"Man rule number two: you don't share a great story over quinoa."

Jimmy shrugs. "We're two blocks from steak. If we're driving we'll have to take your car. Millie's got mine."

"I abandoned my car yesterday. But hey, we're men. We can walk two blocks."

"What do you mean you abandoned your car?"

"I'll tell you at dinner."

They head out the door, walk a block. Mike says, "What's this place called?"

Jimmy points to the sign at the next corner.

Mike reads: "Morning Wood? Is it any good?"

Jimmy grins. "You can't beat Morning Wood."

They enter to find the restaurant busy, work their way to one of the few the empty booths in the bar area, and settle in. Bartender strolls over, asks, "You eating or drinking?"

"Both," Mike says.

"I can take your drink order now, bring the menus later."

They order their bourbons, and Jimmy says, "Before you start, tell me this much: does your story involve a hot girl?"

"You know it does."

"How hot was she?"

"Let me put it this way: her Tampons were made of asbestos!"

Jimmy laughs. "Details, please."

Mike waits for his drink. When it arrives, he sips with reverence, like a guy who knows his bourbon. Jimmy gives him a moment, then says, "You were saying? About the hot girl? What's her name?"

"Brenda."

"Brenda what?"

"Firecrotch."

"Bullshit!"

Mike takes another sip. "You're right, that *was* bullshit. But I'd rather not use real names."

"Fair enough. Wait. Is Brenda a real name?"

"Yeah, sure. It's just not *her* name."

Jimmy shakes his head. "Sorry. It's not the same without her real name. I mean, what's the big deal? Who am *I* gonna tell?"

Mike looks around the room, then says, "Sadie."

"See? I can picture that. Sadie's a helluva lot hotter name than Brenda. So what happened?"

"Friday night I'm in Charlottesville, Highway 27, heading home from happy hour when my car dies."

"Dies how?"

"I don't know. I'm not a mechanic. It just died."

"Did it make a sound first?"

"Engine coughed a couple times, like I had water in the gas line or something."

"You run out of gas?"

Mike gives him a look.

"Course you didn't," Jimmy says. "How far'd you get?"

"Before my car died? Maybe a mile."

"How late was it?"

"What difference does that make?"

"Humor me."

"I don't know. Nine-thirty? Ten? Something like that."

"You always go there? That same restaurant?"

"On Fridays? Yeah. Usually."

"Lotta people know that?"

Mike shrugs.

Jimmy bites the corner of his lip. "You know what I think?"

"No," Mike says. "I only know how *long* it takes you to tell me."

"It sounds like you got potatoed."

"What?"

"Like someone jammed a potato in your exhaust pipe. A clogged tailpipe would shut your car down after a mile or two."

"Why a potato?"

"I mean, it could've been a sock, shorts, a rag, or t-shirt. Anything big enough to clog the pipe. Back in the day we used potatoes."

"Why?"

"It's a time-honored tradition. Potatoes are easy to find, easy to carry, and tend to stay put in a tail pipe."

"What I'm asking, why do that to someone's *car*?"

"Back then? Say we were at a dance and wanted to beat a guy's ass, but wanted to get him alone first. We'd find his car in the parking lot, stick a potato in his tail pipe, follow him from a distance. When he pulled over, we'd pull in behind him and whip his ass."

"You did that a lot?"

"A few times."

Mike frowns.

Jimmy says, "Is that what happened? You pulled over and got jumped?"

"Nah."

"What'd you do, call Triple A?"

"Didn't get a chance."

"Why not?"

"Sadie showed up."

He grins. "Sadie Firecrotch jumped out of her car and whipped your ass?"

Mike gives him a look. "Yeah, that's exactly what happened," he says, sarcastically.

Jimmy laughs again. Then says, "You ever see her before Friday?"

"Nope."

"She just pulled in behind you? Just like that?"

"Just like that."

Jimmy shakes his head. "Sonuva bitch! Then what happened?"

Chapter 2

"SADIE OFFERED ME a ride."

"She *what*? A total *stranger*?"

"She actually wanted *me* to drive *her* car. Said she was stressed out, having a hard time staying in the right lane."

"She trusted you that fast?"

"She had her headlights on me long enough to get a good look. Then she motioned me over, asked my name, made me show my driver's license. But yeah, she trusted me pretty quick. Said I looked big enough for what she had in mind."

"*Big* enough?" Jimmy laughs.

"That's what she said."

"She had her headlights on you and saw what, your Bill Bixby or Incredible Hulk?"

"I have no idea what you're asking me right now."

"I'm asking if you had a hard on."

"What?"

"An erection."

Mike frowns. "My car breaks down, it's dark, I'm on the side of the road, I see headlights, I'm supposed to chub up?"

"Forget that part. So she motions you over, and what, you get behind the wheel?"

Mike nods.

"What was she wearing?"

"Jeans, T-shirt."

"High heels?"

"Flats."

Jimmy winces. "Shit."

"What's wrong?"

"You shoulda said heels."

"Why?"

"I hate flats. Millie wears 'em. They're unsexy as hell."

"Not on *this* woman."

"Jesus, Mike. Something's not right here. Goddesses don't wear flats."

Mike shrugs. "Facts are facts. You want to hear the rest, or are we done?"

"What happened with your car?"

Mike's next sip puts him one from done, so he signals the bartender for another round and says, "I told Sadie I had Triple A, and she said her friend, Craig, towed for them. Said if I called it'd take forever, but if *she* called he'd be there in five."

"She called him?"

"Yeah."

"Let me guess. Craig showed up, pistol-whipped you, and robbed your ass."

"No. Craig told her he'd tow my car back to his station and work on it first thing Saturday morning. She gave him my phone number and said he'd call me when it was ready."

"You left your keys?"

"Yeah. On top of the tire."

"Which one?"

"Front passenger."

Jimmy shakes his head. "She stole your car, didn't she!"

"No. But you're getting ahead of me."

"You should've waited for Craig to show up."

"Yeah, but I didn't want to miss out on Sadie."

Jimmy nods. "Can't blame you for that. So you put your keys on the tire and drove where?"

"Her hotel."

"Wow!"

"At least, that's where she asked me to take her. Unfortunately, we wound up in a blue van."

Before Mike can elaborate, the bartender shows up with two fresh tumblers and says, "You guys heard the latest?"

"About the bombing?" Jimmy says. "Hard to tell. Story changes every time I turn on the TV."

Bartender nods. "People panic, rumors become facts. It takes a few days to sort things out, get a handle on what really happened." He shakes his head. "Sorry sons of bitches. I never thought they'd nuke us on our own soil. I hope they know this means war."

"They'd better. So what's the latest?"

"There's been a second attack."

"No *shit*? Another nuke?"

"No. But they poisoned a waterline."

"Where?"

"Virginia. Same state, different area."

"How bad is it?"

"Sixteen dead, hundreds deathly ill. The whole state's in a panic."

Jimmy says, "When did *that* happen? I was watching TV an hour ago."

"People started getting sick three days ago, but no one pieced it together till they started dropping like flies. Now they say terrorists pumped poison into the water supply. So far it's just one neighborhood, but it could happen anywhere. They're telling people across the country to report any suspicious activities around water companies or fire hydrants."

"Fuckin' terrorists. Planes, nukes, poisoned water. What's next?"

"There's actually some good news," bartender says. "Radiation study's finished. Three miles outside the blast site, levels are virtually zero, thank God."

"Maybe we dodged a bullet," Jimmy says.

Mike waits till the bartender leaves before saying, "*That's* what happened to me."

"What're you talking about?"

"The van that blew up."

"What about it?"

"I was two miles away when it happened."

"In Virginia?"

Mike nods. "That's the blue van I was *in* Friday night."

"With Sadie?"

53

Mike nods. "And I got out just before it blew all to hell."

Jimmy's jaw drops. "You tell the cops?"

Mike shakes his head.

"Why not?"

"Would *you* want to be witness to a fuckin' terrorist act? If these guys can detonate a nuclear weapon fifty miles from the White House they can sure as shit kill *me*! And anyway, I'm not the only one who was in the van that night. The doctors know as much as I do."

"What doctors?"

"The Swingin' Grouchos."

Jimmy gives him a look.

Mike says, "Medical students who play in a band. They—"

Jimmy waves him off. "Let's save that part for later. Tell me about Sadie."

"I don't think she made it."

"What do you mean?"

"I think she was in the van when it blew up. Her and some hillbilly guy."

Jimmy frowns. "I don't believe this."

"What?"

"You've gotta be the worst story teller in the world. The girl *dies*? Jesus! You should've saved that part for later. You really killed the mood."

Mike shrugs.

Jimmy sets his glass on the table and stares at it. Turns it with his hands till it makes a full circle. Then says, "At least tell me you fucked her."

"Sorry to burst your bubble."

"But you were *going* to, right? I mean, why else would she invite you to her hotel?"

"To protect her girlfriend."

"She was gay?"

"No, gutter brain. Her best friend was a girl."

"Protect her from what?"

Chapter 3

"SADIE'S FRIEND MET a wealthy businessman online and agreed to have sex with him for a ton of cash. Sadie was worried something might go wrong."

"Like what?"

Mike thinks a minute. "I don't know. Like maybe the guy that showed up might not be the guy she thought, or maybe he'd turn out to be a creep, or maybe he'd try to hurt her, or not pay her. That sort of thing."

"How much was he gonna pay?"

"Five grand."

"Bullshit! No one's worth five grand."

"*This* girl was. According to Sadie."

"Can't be. Not if she's a hooker."

"She's not a hooker. But for five grand—"

"Right. Who wouldn't?"

"Exactly."

"So what happened?"

"She and her friend had connecting rooms. We'd be in Sadie's room, and the connecting doors would be slightly open so we could hear what was happening. If things went bad for Sadie's friend, we'd burst in and protect her."

"You weren't worried they were setting you up?"

"No. She was definitely scared. I believed her."

"So you started driving to the hotel, but wound up in the van?"

"Yeah."

"How'd that happen?"

"We got kidnapped."

Jimmy's eyes grow wide. "Holy shit! Wait. You swear this is true?"

"Swear to God."

"How'd someone kidnap you while you were driving?"

"Sadie didn't know it, but someone had put cameras in her car. While I'm driving her to the hotel this guy started talking to us through a speaker. Said he'd kill us if we didn't do what he said."

Jimmy frowns. "C'mon, Mike. Talking *cars*? *Cameras*?"

"It's true!" Mike says. "I nearly shit my pants." He notes the skeptical look on Jimmy's face and says, "You know those TV shows where they rig cars with hidden cameras and wait till crooks steal them?"

"Like *Dateline*, or whatever?"

"You've seen that, right? The kids jack the car, start driving, suddenly the sound comes on and the TV guy starts talking to them? They can even shut the cars down remotely."

"Yeah, I've seen those shows. So who was the guy?"

Chapter 4

MIKE LOOKS AROUND, lowers his voice. "I assume he was one of the terrorists. He told us to drive to a certain place, park the car, and a blue van would pick us up."

"You saw them? The terrorists?"

"Just the one in the van."

Jimmy's eyes grow wide. "You can *identify* him?"

"I should damn-well *hope* so. I was with him the better part of an hour."

"Wait. Is that why you abandoned your car?"

Mike nods. "Took me days to hitchhike here."

"No fuckin' way!"

"It's true."

"No. I mean, no fuckin' way are you staying at my place."

"Two days is all I need," Mike says. "There's no way they can find me in two days."

"Sorry."

"How about one night? C'mon, Jimmy. I'm in a bind."

"Out of the question." He looks around the room carefully, seeking terrorists. "I shouldn't even be here with you."

"There's nothing to worry about. If I thought there was, I sure as shit wouldn't be here myself. First of all, the terrorist is dead. I doubt anyone even knows I was *in* the van that night."

"I'm not stupid, Mike."

"What do you mean?"

"Your life's in danger. You left town, showed up on my doorstep. You may not be worried about the terrorist that's dead, but you're sure as hell worried about the one you talked to in the car, on the speaker."

Mike says, "Wouldn't *you* be?"

"Of course. I'm even scared for *myself*, just being in public with you."

"Then imagine how *I* feel! Let me stay the night, Jimmy. Just tonight. I'll leave first thing in the morning, and you'll never have to see me again."

"If it was just me, it'd be different. Maybe. But I can't put Millie in danger."

"She doesn't have to know."

"Yeah, Mike, she does. I'm sorry."

They're quiet till Jimmy says, "You saw the bomb?"

"Yeah. At the time it didn't register. I just thought it was scrap iron and shit."

"They said they were gonna blow up the White House?"

"No, but that's what I realized after the fact."

"*Jesus*, Mike! You need to *tell* someone!"

"If the Grouchos come through, I won't have to."

A voice behind them says, "Scoot over, Mike."

"*Shit!*" Mike says. He jumps to his feet, but a giant hand pushes him back onto the bench with authority. Jimmy starts to make a move, but finds himself staring at a badge he could have sworn wasn't in the big guy's hand a second earlier.

The guy says, "Move closer to the wall, and stay put." Then he pushes Mike against the wall so he's directly opposite Jimmy. He sits beside Mike and says, "Jimmy? I'm Donovan Creed, Homeland Security. Congratulations. Your friend just bought you three years of unprecedented government scrutiny."

Jimmy studies the badge. "What do you mean?"

"You and your wife just made front page, Terrorist Watch List."

"*What?*"

"For the next three years, every facet of your life will be under a microscope." He watches Jimmy a moment, then adds, "I see you sitting there, hearing me say this, but you have no idea what it truly means. How intrusive we're going to be. Everywhere you and Millie go...everything you do...everyone with whom you associate...every phone call, text...every keystroke ever made on any computer you've touched or *will* touch—will be recorded and analyzed by a team of experts."

"You can't threaten us! We're American citizens."

"Here's the funny thing, Jimmy: if you *weren't* American citizens, we wouldn't be *allowed* to do this!"

"How'd you know my wife's name? Who the fuck *are* you?"

"I already told you. Donovan Creed."

"You're going to *spy* on us? What, with hidden *cameras*? Recording devices?"

Creed shakes his head. "You really don't have a clue how this works, do you? Let me put it bluntly: for the next three years, every time Millie has a bowel movement, we'll know the volume, texture, and composition."

"That's disgusting. Not to mention impossible."

"It's not only possible, it's your new normal. On the bright side, if our people do their jobs properly, you and Millie will never know the difference. But say one word about this to her or anyone else, or mention Mike's name, or mine, you'll find yourself in an underground facility so secret only sixty people on earth know about it, and forty of them are prisoners."

"I'll say whatever the fuck I want to whoever I want. I'm a citizen, with rights."

"Your rights ended the minute Mike gave you Sadie's name. If he'd given you her last name, you'd be dead right now."

Mike says, "I don't even know her last name."

"Which is the only reason *you're* still alive," Creed says.

"I'm not involved in this," Jimmy says. "I haven't seen this guy for years. Have no knowledge of his activities, and anyway, he's a witness, not a terrorist."

"You're not listening, Jimmy," Creed says. "But you should." He reaches into his jacket, hands Jimmy a pair of panties. "Recognize these?"

"Not really."

"Millie will. They're hers."

"You've been in my fuckin' *house*?"

"Our people are there right now, sifting through your computers, matching your interior paint colors."

"What the fuck are you talking about?"

"You've never heard of smart paint? Imbedded sensors that transmit video and sound? One day next week you'll come home and won't even realize we've painted little sections of your house. No more secrets, Jimmy, no more privacy. Within twenty-four hours we'll know everything you've ever done and everything you're *going* to do."

Jimmy grabs his cell phone.

Creed says, "Make that call and you'll regret it. Want instant proof?"

"I'm not calling the cops. I'm calling Millie. She's on her way home. If she sees people in our house, she'll freak."

"They'll be gone before she gets home. Here's how I know."

Creed produces his phone, tilts it so Jimmy can see. "Recognize this car? It's yours. Millie's driving. When you give the word, she'll experience a flat tire. Say when."

"That's insane. This is obviously some sort of joke. You couldn't have found her this quickly."

"Say the word, Jimmy. She's about to hit the freeway. A flat could be deadly."

"Fuck you! This is complete bullshit."

"Fine, I'll make the decision for you. How about...*now!*" Creed presses a key, puts the phone in his pocket and says, "When she calls, act surprised. Tell her who to call to get her tire fixed, and remember not to say a word about any of this."

Jimmy's phone rings. He answers and does his best to calm Millie down. When he ends the call, Creed places a hundred dollar bill on the table, secures it with Mike's bourbon glass, and says, "Here's what's going to happen: the three of us are going to get up and walk out of here like old friends with someplace to go."

Jimmy stares straight ahead. "You shot my wife's tire out by pressing a *button?*"

"My people did the heavy lifting on that."

"You don't work for Homeland Security."

"Well, no. Not officially."

"You're some sort of shakedown artist. To begin with, I don't believe those are Millie's panties."

"Don't beat yourself up about that, Jimmy. I bet you'd recognize them if your sex life was better."

"Fuck you, Creed! I don't know how you pulled off the tire thing, but I noticed you turned your phone off the minute you pressed the button. If you'd really blown out her tire in real time you'd have shown it happening. As for everything else you said? Total bullshit. I happen to know the government doesn't work that way."

"You require more proof?"

"Let's just say it'll take a lot more than a pair of panties and a flat tire to send me runnin' home scared."

"What if I kill someone for you? Would that help convince you?"

Jimmy laughs. "Yeah, sure, go ahead. Kill someone. Knock yourself out."

"It'll be on your conscience."

"I can deal with it."

Creed produces a tube of lip balm from his pocket, removes the cap, dabs some gel on the C note. Wads up a cocktail napkin, uses it to spread the gel across the face of the bill. Then says, "Bartender seems like a nice guy. I hate to see him die for such a stupid reason."

Jimmy laughs. "I'm supposed to believe when he touches the money he's gonna die?"

"Not immediately, but yeah, within the hour. It's a contact poison."

"That, my friend, is total bullshit."

"Tell you what: we'll leave, you can come back in an hour and check on him. But be smart about it, or they'll think you were involved."

Jimmy says, "Here's what I think of your bullshit." He grabs the bill, stuffs it in his pocket. Says, "Fuck you both."

Creed watches him leave, then presses a key on his phone. When someone on the other end answers, he says, "We're done. Grab your stuff and go. Problem solved."

Mike says, "What happened?"

"Jimmy just saved us three years of hard work."

"You *killed* him?"

"He killed himself. I don't think I've never met such a bad listener." He puts another C note on the table and says, "Let's go."

"Wh-where are you t-taking me?"

"Same place I told Jimmy about."

"That underground p-prison thing? It's real?"

"Very."

"F-For how long?"

"Till your coping skills run out."

"H-How did you f-find me so quickly?"

"Like you said: the Grouchos came through."

PART FOUR:
Donovan Creed

Chapter 1

Three Days Earlier...

SHE WAS YOUNG, the room was cold; her nipples were as puckered as a grandmother's kiss. She moved beneath me gracefully, with a tenderness only a gifted poet could describe. We made love slowly, with reverence, by candlelight.

Afterward, she cried like Jimmy Swaggart, peeling onions.

But in a good way.

Her name was—*is*—Trudy Lake, and I'm Donovan Creed. If I told you more about that night with Trudy, you'd wet your pants.

I certainly did.

I'd tell you anyway, but Callie Carpenter just entered the room. Callie's an assassin, part of my Sensory Resources team. For years she and I—and a dozen other crazies—killed terrorists for Uncle Sam. These days I devise terrorist

69

scenarios for Homeland Security and she and I perform the occasional freelance hit for organized crime. Not for the money, but to stay sharp because...well, that's what we do. We kill people, and we're damn good at it, and smart enough to know if we're *not* killing people, somewhere in the world someone else *is*. And when we eventually meet them, Callie and I will either be ready, or we'll be dead.

She's here to deliver some big secret about Miranda Rodriguez. Arrived an hour ago, said she wanted to deliver the news in person to see the look on my face when she tells me. I played it cool, told her to relax; unpack her suitcase, get cleaned up for lunch.

She did, and now she's here, in the den of my fortress saying, "You're looking well, Donovan."

What she really means is I look a helluva lot better than the last time she saw me, which was at my daughter Kimberly's funeral last year. Of course, Callie looks just as you'd expect: amazing.

No, better than that.

I'll risk accusations of hyperbole and tell you flat-out that Callie's looks are unrivaled on the planet Earth. Go ahead: roll your eyes. But if you were standing beside me right now, checking her out, you'd not only agree, but you'd add the entire universe for good measure: all contents of intergalactic space, from the smallest subatomic particle to the largest reservoir of matter and energy.

"You look good too," I say, demonstrating my capacity for understatement.

She says, "Are you seeing anyone?"

"I am."

She arches a perfect brow. "Is it someone I know?"

"I hope not!"

Last year my romantic relationship with Callie went toxic faster than David Lee Roth's radio show, sending us death-spiraling into madness. One reason? She murdered my former fiancée. I toss a couple ice cubes in her drink and say, "Tell me your news."

Chapter 2

"YOU REMEMBER MIRANDA," Callie says, slyly.

I show her a thin smile. As Callie is acutely aware, Miranda Rodriguez had been my favorite hooker from date number one till the day she got her master's in counseling psychology, at which point she quit whoring. Callie also knows I offered Miranda a fortune to work for us at Sensory Resources as a facilitator. Miranda agreed, but asked me to wait a year so she could travel the world.

The year came and went and so did Miranda, and I never heard from her again.

"Callie?"

"Yeah?"

"How long have we known each other?"

She studies my face. "Why do you ask?"

"You're holding your drink unusually high."

"I thought it wise, under the circumstances."

"I also notice your knees are slightly bent."

"So?"

"Your torso's angled to present a smaller target."

"Anything else?"

"Your core is perfectly balanced."

"Thank you. Your point?"

"Are you expecting an attack?"

"I considered it one of several possible reactions you might have."

"To the news about Miranda?"

She nods.

"I had the impression you were bringing me *good* news."

"*I* think it's good," she says. "But you might take exception."

"To what?"

"My delay in sharing it."

"How long have you been sitting on this information?"

"A year, give or take."

She waits for me to say something. When I don't, she says, "Remember when we were in Manhattan last year and you met Gideon and Kathleen for dinner at the Four Seasons?"

I do, and motion her to continue.

She says, "You stationed me in front of the restaurant and had me monitor your conversation on my cell phone."

"And?"

"I happened to see Miranda crossing Park Avenue at East 52nd with your witchy friend, Rose. Uh..." She thinks a moment. "I can't recall Rose's last name."

"Stout."

She cocks her head. "*Stout?* You're sure?"

I nod.

"Thanks. That would have bothered me all night and I never *would* have gotten it."

"Miranda and Rose were together? You're certain?"

"Yes." She locks her eyes on mine and says, "Miranda was pregnant."

She pauses in case I want to do the math.

"This was a year ago?"

"Approximately."

"And how pregnant was she at the time?"

"Picture Kim Kardashian's ass on my stomach."

"I'd rather not."

Callie frowns. "Me either. But since we've broached the Gates of Gross, I'll ask how could you *possibly* have had sex with that woman?"

"Why not? She's brilliant, funny, gorgeous...."

"She's fucked half the men in New York!"

"Exaggerate much?"

"My bad. Half the *wealthy* men. So how stretched out *was* she? I mean, could you even *feel* her when you fucked her? Or was it like heaving a hotdog into Mammoth Cave?"

"How about we get back on track? Why didn't you tell me you saw Miranda that day? Or any time during the past year?"

"It was a tough call. Every day I wanted to tell you, and every week I asked myself why I hadn't."

"That doesn't sound like you."

"Are you kidding? I asked *why* more times than Nancy Kerrigan, when that guy smashed her leg with a pipe."

"Police baton."

"Whatever."

"Look, I knew you had a right to know, but we were in the early stages of our relationship and I didn't want to lose you."

"And why would that have happened?"

"Because I knew you were the father."

Chapter 3

"LIKE YOU SAID, Miranda was a hooker. I bet twenty men could claim paternity."

"It's your baby, Donovan. I'm certain."

"She told you?"

"No. But when I tried to approach them, Rose did something to me. With her mind."

I start humming the theme to Twilight Zone, but Callie says, "I know it sounds crazy, but Rose stared at me a certain way, and...I couldn't move. I froze like a statue. Then I felt her planting thoughts in my head."

"What kind of thoughts?"

"It was like...she was trying to make me forget Miranda was pregnant. Or that I'd seen her at all."

Callie notes my expression, then shakes her head. "You bastard!"

"What?"

"I don't believe it. You already knew."

I smile.

"But how?" she says.

I reach for my pocket, but before my hand gets there I notice the knife in Callie's left hand. That's how quick she is. First, there's nothing. Then she's holding a knife or gun. Then you're dead.

"I'm just getting my cell phone," I say.

"The one that's equipped with an explosive device?"

"Well, sure, but—"

"You press a button, fling it at me, and blow my ass to hell? No thanks."

"You think I'd blow you up in my own den? Don't be silly. And anyway, your phone has the same capability."

"Yeah, but I'm more accurate with the knife."

"Put it away, Callie. I would never hurt you."

"I believe you completely. But how stupid would I feel if you proved me wrong?"

I press a key—not the button Callie's talking about—on my phone. When Trudy answers, I say, "Callie's here. Want to meet her?"

Keeping a close eye on each other, Callie and I slowly pocket our weapons. Seconds later, Trudy enters the room with a baby in one arm, a carrier in the other. She places the baby in the carrier, then sets it on the floor.

"Callie, I'd like you to meet Trudy and Hawley."

Callie takes a step closer to them. "Which is which?"

"Hawley's the baby."

"Miranda's baby?"

Trudy looks at me nervously.

Callie cocks her head. "Donovan? What happened to Miranda?"

"I have no idea."

"You didn't...ah..."

"No."

"Have you tried to find her?"

"No."

Callie shifts her focus to Trudy. "You're the babysitter?"

"No, ma'am."

Callie recoils in horror. "Did you just call me *ma'am?*"

"Sorry," Trudy says. "It's a habit."

Callie frowns. "If you're not the babysitter, who are you?"

"The wife."

"*Who's* wife?"

Trudy points at me.

Callie's jaw drops. "*What?*"

Chapter 4

CALLIE SPITS THE words: "You're...*married?*"

I grin. "We are."

"Since when?"

"Two weeks last Saturday."

"We haven't honeymooned yet," Trudy says, approaching Callie with her hand extended.

Callie says, "I don't shake hands."

"I should a' realized that," Trudy says. "Donovan don't shake hands, neither. He says it's a good way to get stabbed. I do hope we can be friends, though, and maybe then you'll give me a big 'ol hug."

"A hug?"

"I'd like that, if it suits you."

Callie looks at me. "So many questions come to mind."

"Such as?"

"Who *is* this person? And who *talks* like this in the current century? And if she's *here*, who's minding her trailer?

And how'd she get here in the *first* place? I didn't see a swamp boat, tractor, or hay baler parked out front."

I smile. "The answers are Trudy, she's from rural Kentucky, there's no trailer involved, and she arrived by limo, at my invitation. And just so you know, I happen to love the way she talks."

Trudy shows me a radiant, grateful smile.

Callie sees it and frowns. Turns to Trudy and says, "You want me to *hug* you?"

"Yes ma'am, someday, if it's your wish. But soon, I hope, since you're practically family and all."

I say, "She's right. You are."

"And yet I wasn't invited to the wedding."

"It was a private ceremony. Just the two of us and a minister. Anson witnessed."

Callie stares Trudy up and down, as if trying to guess her weight. Then asks, "How *old* are you?"

"Double digits."

"That's comforting."

Trudy gives me a wink and says, "Donovan and I are connected on a level that transcends age."

"Those sound like *his* words, not yours."

"Those *are* his words. But I feel the same way. Age is just a number."

"I agree. What's yours?"

"It varies."

"What are you planning to tell the truant officer?"

"We agreed to tell folks I'm practically twenty-one."

Callie offers a skeptical look. "I'd say eighteen would be a stretch."

"Oh, I expect I'm at *least* eighteen!"

"You *expect?* Are you saying you don't know your own *age?*"

"Not for certain."

"How's that possible?"

"My parents agreed I was born on a Saturday, but always argued over which year."

"I'm sure the hospital records could settle it."

"I weren't born in a hospital."

"No?"

"I was born in a duck blind near Clover Fork, on the Cumberland River."

"A *duck* blind?"

"My parents were on the run on account a' Daddy bein' neck-deep in his moonshine phase. Years passed before he settled us in Clayton and got around to fillin' out the birth forms so I could enter first grade."

"You were born in a *duck* blind?"

"That's where my parents were hidin' when my mom's water broke." She smiles, changes the subject: "Donovan *said* you were gorgeous, but you're *way* past that!"

Callie stares at her blankly.

"I *mean* it, Callie. You're the most beautiful woman I ever saw."

Callie struggles to form a compliment of her own, gives up, and asks, "Are you really married?"

Trudy nods.

"To Creed?"

"Yes ma'am."

Callie looks at me, shakes her head. "And all this time I thought Dennis Rodman was the king of rebounds."

"This isn't a rebound," I say. "Trudy's a force of nature."

"I agree she's one of a kind. Far prettier than the others I've seen you with over the years, though I *do* hate the thought of her wasting that willowy, athletic body on a man. Especially one whose better days are behind him."

Trudy speaks up: "I've got no complaints, Callie. He's all the man I'll ever need."

Callie laughs derisively. "Oh really? Wow, what a shock! You're saying being married to Donovan Creed—a billionaire—is a step up from *pig* farming? Yeah, I agree."

Trudy looks down a moment, then slowly lifts her chin and displays a look of such total innocence and beauty you'd swear you were looking at a 20-year-old Michelle Phillips. She says, "I'll admit I come from what you'd call white trash. But I always had flowers."

"I'm not familiar with that expression."

"It's not one, far as I know. I'm just sayin', no matter how poor I was, or how shabby my livin' arrangements, I always had fresh flowers in the house. It may not be a big thing, but it stands for one. And Callie?"

"Yeah?"

"You, of all people, should know that bein' born badly ain't an excuse for stayin' that way. You overcame your childhood, and I'm tryin' to do the same. I may be ignorant, but that's a temporary situation. I'm a lot smarter than you think."

"You're not just smart, Trudy. You're brilliant."

"Excuse me?"

"Lots of people are smart. *I'm* smart. But *you're* brilliant as hell! Creed is *not* the marrying type."

"If that's a compliment, it's a right-nice one. But you've still got me beat."

"How so?"

"I'd rather be smart and drop-dead gorgeous than brilliant as hell."

"Why's that?"

"In my experience it's a rare man who'll slide his hand down a woman's bra hopin' to find her report card."

"Does that mean you're feeling threatened by me?"

"No ma'am."

"Surely you're jealous."

"Not really."

"Perhaps you *should* be. Donovan and I have quite a history."

"I know."

"We've...*slept* together."

Trudy nods. "I know."

"We've had *sex*, Trudy."

"I've had sex before *too*, Callie, but Donovan don't fault me for my past."

"You've told him *everything?*"

"I've told him very little. But only because he hasn't asked."

Trudy's phone rings. She glances at it, frowns, then takes the call: "This is Trudy. Who's this?" She listens a moment and says, "Merle, I don't even know what that means, but even if I did, I wouldn't care to try it with anyone but my husband." She listens some more before saying, "Well, thanks for the compliment, but you shouldn't waste your call on me. You should be callin' your mom, or grandma....Nope, sorry, I can't do that, neither, but I'd be happy to pray for your salvation if you like....Well, okay then, be safe. Bye."

When she ends the call, Callie says, "Has Donovan shared any of *his* sexual history with *you?*"

"He's told me all I need to know."

"*That* must have been a long conversation!"

"Not really. I only asked him about his serious relationships."

Callie arches a brow. "How many women made that list?"

"Four."

"His first wife."

Trudy nods.

"Kathleen."

Trudy nods again.

"Me."

"Of course."

Callie looks at me. "Who's the fourth?"

"I'd rather not say."

"Beth Conroy?"

Trudy cocks her head and gives me a look that says she should have heard that name from me, not Callie. I set things straight by saying, "Beth and I never had a sexual relationship."

Callie smiles. "Thanks for clearing that up. I always suspected Beth was the one that got away."

With the full weight of Trudy's eyes on my face I say, "Beth and I were never intimate. It was her choice, and I respected it. I haven't seen or heard from her since."

Callie says, "If that's true, the fourth has to be Rachel Case, who's fifty shades of grief. If I were you, Trudy, I'd ask him about the others. There's a lot of history in his pants. Things you'll want to know."

"Thanks, Callie," I say.

Trudy says, "I'm not interested in the others. Donovan's the type of man any woman would want to curl up with. From day one I knew I could throw a cat in any direction and hit a woman he's slept with, but that don't mean I wouldn't welcome her as a friend." She holds Callie's gaze before adding, "Long as she don't cross the line."

"Your husband and I will be spending countless days and nights together working on cases."

Trudy looks at me. "Is that true?"

I nod.

She sets her jaw and says, "That's okay. I trust Donovan. He won't stray."

"You're sure about that?"

"Totally. And I'm pleased to hear it's you who'll be with him all those days and nights."

"Why?" Callie says, clearly surprised.

"Because even though Donovan loves me truly, there are lots of women who'd line up to offer him temptations. But if you're with him they'll figure they got no chance. I know I can count on you to help keep him on the straight and narrow when we're apart."

Callie smirks. "Why would I do that?"

"Because you and Donovan have deep feelin's for each other and you'll want what's best for him."

"Meaning you?"

"Meanin' me and Hawley."

Callie weighs her words before saying, "I may have mis-judged you. That's a major compliment, by the way."

"Thanks, Callie."

"Are you saying you'd leave him if he cheats on you?"

"Yes, of course. Hawley and I won't cuss him, or wish him ill, but we'll leave. And he knows it."

Callie says, "You're aware Donovan was a spy? He's very good at covering things up. To put it bluntly, if he decides to cheat, you'd never know."

"Maybe *I* won't, but Hawley will. And she'll tell me."

Callie glances at the baby. "I'm no expert on infants, but I doubt she's old enough to verbalize a single word."

"She talks with her mind."

Callie rolls her eyes.

Trudy says, "Hawley and I are connected. We know the moon songs."

"Excuse me?"

"The moon?"

"What about it?"

"The moon hums lots of songs, but few can hear 'em."

Callie pauses a moment before saying, "You believe the moon hums songs?"

"I surely do."

"Well, if I were you I wouldn't say that in public, and bear in mind, I'm clinically insane. But apart from that I can assure you Creed would never allow you to walk away with his baby."

"He won't have a choice."

"Why's that?"

"Hawley picked me to raise her."

"Even if we pretend that's true, it's simple physics: Creed's bigger and stronger than you."

"No one's big or strong enough to take Hawley against her will."

Callie laughs.

Trudy says, "Try it, if you don't believe me."

"Try what?"

"Try to pick her up and walk off with her."

Callie shrugs, walks over to the carrier, grabs the handle, attempts to lift it, but it won't budge. She frowns and pulls so hard the handle breaks off the base. She leans down, grips both ends of the carrier, uses her legs for leverage. Though she pulls with all her might, the carrier stays put.

Callie straightens up. "Nice trick. I assume there's some sort of hook or magnet attached to the bottom."

Trudy picks up the handle, reattaches it to the carrier; lifts it with ease. Callie immediately inspects the bottom of the carrier, then checks the floor, but finds nothing.

"As I say, it's a nice trick."

"It's no trick," Trudy says. "It's Hawley's will."

Callie gives her a condescending look. "I'm sure that's it."

"Trudy's right about the baby," I say. "Hawley's unique."

"All parents think their kids are special," Callie sniffs.

Trudy and I exchange a look. Though our faces are neutral, our eyes are smiling. We know Callie's rudeness has nothing to do with Trudy or Hawley, and everything to do with me being married. Callie doesn't *want* me, but doesn't want anyone *else* to have me, either.

Trudy's phone rings again. She checks the display and sighs. "This is Trudy, who's this? Oh, hi Warren. Yeah, that's my picture, but....Well, thanks for the compliment, but I'm not that kind of girl. What are you in for? ....Oh, okay. That explains a lot....No, I'll have to pass on that one, too....Yes I'm sure! I'm married, Warren. And even if I weren't, that's not somethin' I'd do. I mean, I'm not even sure it's physically *possible*. But I'll pray for your godless soul, if you like....Well, the offer stands anyway. Okay then, bye."

Callie says, "What's with all the phone calls?"

Trudy says, "My ex-husband weren't pleased to learn I got remarried."

"So?"

"Out of spite, he posted my picture and phone number on a national prison dating site."

"You're *divorced*?"

"I was, but now I'm married. Which is why Darrell's so pissed."

"How old were you the first time, *twelve*?"

Trudy shrugs.

I say, "Callie? Want to have some fun?"

She gives me a look. "What do you have in mind?"

"Taking a shot at the president."

"The president of what?"

"The United States."

"What kind of shot?"
"Small caliber rifle."

Chapter 5

"YOU'RE GOING TO shoot the president?"

"Not really. I'm just planning to scare the shit out of him."

"When?"

"Now, if you want."

Trudy says, "Well, Hawley and I better get started on lunch. When you guys are done shootin' the president, be sure to come hungry."

"You cook?" Callie says.

I smile. "You'll be amazed what Trudy can do in the kitchen."

"Cute as she is, I'd like to see that. Unless you're talking about actual cooking, in which case I feel compelled to inform you I'm allergic to possum."

"Darn!" Trudy says, laughing. "Oh well, our pantry runs deep. I'll come up with somethin'."

When she's gone, Callie says, "What am I missing?"

"She'll grow on you. You'll see."

"I couldn't warm up to her if we were cremated together."

"You'll see. In the meantime, come with me."

As we descend the steps to my war room, Callie says, "You faked the wedding ceremony. Pretended to marry her so you could get in her pants, right?"

"Nope."

"You're really, seriously married?"

"I really, seriously am."

"To *her?*"

I nod.

She shakes her head. "It's like if James Bond married Elly May Clampett, or one of those Petticoat Junction hillbillies. It can't possibly work," she says.

I smile.

As we enter my war room, she says, "How could you possibly let this happen?"

Chapter 6

HOW COULD I let this happen indeed!

Should I tell Callie the centerpiece of our relationship was dog shit? Because that's how it started one morning, nearly a year ago, while I was working out. I'd barely made a dent in the heavy bag when my cell phone buzzed high alert. Anson, my majordomo, said, "Sorry to disturb you, Mr. Creed. There's been a mild security breach. We're on it."

"There's no such thing as a mild security breach," I said. "What happened?"

"It's the new girl. Trudy Lake."

"What about her?"

"She's taking her first walk around the grounds."

"Under your supervision?"

"Yes, sir."

"That seems harmless enough. What triggered the alarm?"

"She picked up one of the dog droppings."

"Why?"

"I'm...not sure."

I sighed. "On my way."

I found Anson on the front porch, but seeing Trudy on the grounds, I waved him off and headed straight for her. As I closed the distance I asked, "What's your fascination with dog shit?"

"I wouldn't call it fascination, Mr. Creed, I just like to check things out when they don't match up."

"And how did you determine the dog shit doesn't match up? There's more than one dog on the property, Miss Lake."

"Includin' you?" she said, smiling.

I felt my frown change to a small smile.

Hers was big, and covered her face.

"Please," she said. "Call me Trudy."

"Are we to be friends?"

"I hope so."

"Then Trudy it is."

"You're lookin' at me funny," she said.

"Actually, I'm looking at you in a whole new way."

"Don't make too much outta callin' me Trudy. It's just the way you said Miss Lake sounds a lot like *mistake*."

I laughed. "May I walk with you a moment?"

"I'd welcome it."

We traveled about ten feet before Anson interrupted us, moving quickly, extending a phone. I showed him a severe frown, but he said, "Sir, it's the vice president."

Trudy studied the phone with interest till I said, "Tell him I'm busy," at which point she gave me a skeptical look.

I said, "You think we're faking the call? Trying to impress you?"

"Are you?"

"Anson, please put the phone on speaker." He did, and we heard the vice president say, "Donovan? Are you ready to come back to work?"

"I'm not on vacation, Ben. I quit, remember?"

"Well, that's ridiculous. The president asked me to invite you to play golf with him at Camp David tomorrow."

"Tell him no thanks."

"Why not?"

"I don't play golf."

"Everyone plays golf."

"Then it shouldn't be hard to find another player."

"You need to come. He has a proposal for you."

"Sorry. There are a million ways to get killed on a golf course."

The V.P. sighed. "The course will be under total lockdown. If the president's safe, you'll be safe."

"Not true, Ben. I have more enemies than the president."

"That's ridiculous."

"Sorry, it's a no for me."

"He won't be happy to hear it."

"Maybe Decker will play with him."

The Vice President paused, then said, "You really need to be the bigger man here, Creed. Decker's no saint, but we're all on the same side now."

"He caused my daughter's death."

"By mistake."

"He was murdering civilians in their homes and yes, she happened to be in one of them at the time. You call it a mistake, I call it terrorism. The man's a terrorist, and you paid him a hundred million to stop killing Americans."

"That's all water under the bridge. We paid *you* the same amount, as I recall."

"I wasn't paid to stop killing Americans."

"You've killed your share, from what I'm told. Look, let's not quibble over intent. Uncle Sam paid you a fortune for your expertise, and the president expects access."

"Then tell him to come here. It's a helluva lot safer than Camp David."

The V.P. sighed. "I'll pass your message along to the president."

"While you're at it, how about asking him why he refuses to implement the changes I've recommended."

"I can answer that. He thinks your scenarios are far-fetched, and your countermeasures would cause a national panic."

"He's an asshole. He pays me to figure out all the ways terrorists can attack us, but refuses to implement the countermeasures I devise to prevent the attacks. As for being far-fetched, I've never sent you guys a scenario I couldn't personally implement."

"Well, I'm inclined to believe you, but it's not up to me, is it?"

"Apparently not. But someday I'd love to hear what vice presidents *are* allowed to do, beyond arranging golf dates and dinner parties."

"Me too!" he said, laughing.

When Anson ended the call Trudy said, "That was *him*! Ben Campbell! I've heard him on TV. Same voice!"

I said, "Why did you think the dog shit looked out of place?"

She took a moment before saying, "Am I the first to notice that?"

"You are."

"Guess you don't have many Southern girls walkin' your property."

"That's true. And it's a pity."

"You like Southern girls, do you?"

"It's a weakness."

"I'd call it a strength. *Aha!*"

"What now?"

"I caught you smilin' for real. You've got a nice one."

"Thanks. What about the dog shit?"

She stopped walking. "Do you really expect me to believe you don't know there are six stacks of fake dog doo on your property?"

"No. But I want you to tell me how you figured it out so quickly. And if you have any idea what they're for."

"Number one, there shouldn't be *any* dog doo in the yard of an estate like this. It shows poor gardenin'."

"It's not like they're out in the open."

"That's another thing. Dogs are sorta particular about where they do their business. All six piles were in shady spots. Dogs are more apt to squat in sunshine."

"I doubt that's a universal fact."

"I'll accept Yankee dogs might act differently. Yankee *people* sure do!"

"We're hardly Yankees. This is Virginia. And I grew up in the South."

"If that's true you're not very observant about dog behavior."

"What are you, an expert?"

"No, but I know a lot of animal facts."

"Such as?"

"Don't get me started. Last time someone asked me that I wound up knockin' her naked at a dinner party."

I gave her a long look. "I wish I'd been there to see *that!*"

"I bet you would!"

"Let's talk about the dog shit."

"The *fake* dog shit."

"You said shit."

"I tried to be more genteel, but you weren't havin' none of it."

"Sorry," I said. "I engage in a crude line of work, and my speech tends to reflect it."

"That's okay. I have a vulgar side myself. It comes out when I'm angry or in the throes."

"Is that what tipped you off? The dog droppings shouldn't be present on an estate like this and they were all in shady spots?"

"That's part of it...but the plain fact is they don't look quite right."

"How so? These droppings were given perfect marks by highly-respected dog breeders."

"Highly-*respected? Seriously? Omigod!* Yankees really *are* crazy!"

"What are you *talking* about?"

"Where I come from *no one* respects them that fornicate with dogs!"

"The kind of dog breeders I'm talking about don't actually have sex with dogs."

"You know that for a fact?"

I studied her face. "Why Trudy Lake, I do believe you're messin' with me."

She grinned. "Ya think?"

And just like that, I was smitten. Neither of us was looking for love, but from that moment on we were two stones caught in an avalanche. I don't think Trudy realized it at the time, because all she said was, "Small town Southern girls know their dog shit. We have to shovel enough of it off our lawns each day, and it don't take long to figure out which dogs makes which piles. I've turned my hose on half the dogs in the county to keep 'em from fuckin' the other half, and used that same hose to clean up more shit than a congressional aide."

I said, "From here on out I'm going to stop apologizing for my colorful language."

She smiled. "I'd be the last person on earth to ask a man to change his style of talkin'."

"Very well. Have you discerned the purpose of my fake dog shit?"

"They've got tiny cameras on four sides, and are hollow inside. You probably use 'em to spy on people and hide stuff in, like keys, or thumb drives."

She was right.

Now, present day, with Callie sitting beside me watching the computer monitor, I say, "The president refuses to believe how easy he could be killed at Camp David."

"So you're going to show him?"

"Yup."

"By shooting at him?"

"Yup."

"Is that wise?"

"Probably not."

"In that case, count me in!"

Chapter 7

I NEVER MET the president for golf last year, but I got his attention on the phone one day by saying, "When you end this call, Mr. President, ask your smart phone which planes are flying over your head right now."

"Why?"

"Because within five seconds you'll see a display of every airline flying above you, including flight numbers, types of aircraft, altitudes, angles, and slant distances. The information will be slightly delayed, but it's easy enough to track these planes live if you know what you're doing."

"Bullshit."

"Give it a try."

He did, and was as stunned as you'll be if you've never tried it. In fact, go ahead and try it now. Got an iPhone? Ask Siri, "Which planes are flying over my head right now?"

I'll pause while you do it.

Astonishing, isn't it? And that's just the tip of the security iceberg.

Want to see something even scarier?

Download the PlaneFinder AR iOS app and hold it skyward. Within seconds little blue squares will pop up showing you where the planes are, along with the flight information. Cool, if you're two miles from the airport and want to identify Aunt Nelda's actual plane before she lands. Not so cool if you're a terrorist with a stinger missile who wants to send Aunt Nelda to hell for posting a photo of pork-laced bullets on her Facebook page (I'm not making this up about the pork-laced bullets. A company in Idaho coats bullets in pork-infused paint for those who not only want to *kill* Islamic terrorists, but also prevent them from entering paradise).

But I digress. My point is this: if every man, woman, and child with a cell phone can identify the planes above us, imagine how easy it would be for terrorists to obtain or create technology capable of killing high-profile individuals from a distance.

Even the president.

Callie says, "Correct me if I'm wrong, but I've studied topography maps of Camp David, and—"

"Why?"

"In case you ever ask me to assassinate the president."

"You think you could?"

She smiles. "Are you asking me to?"

"No."

"Well, anyway, there's no golf course there."

"You're right. There's no room for an *actual* golf course. But there's a one-hole course Robert Trent Jones designed a million years ago, with an Augusta-type green, and four tee boxes that range from 80 to 140 yards. You hit four balls, one from each tee, then walk down to the green and putt them in. Then you climb back up the terrace and hit four more."

"Thanks, Mr. Wizard, for making me yawn."

"My pleasure."

"Let's skip to the plan."

"Okay. Remember Decker's predator drones? The ones he tried to bomb the crowd with at the fireworks display?"

"I remember his plan failed."

"Yes. But only because he tried to fly a dozen in tandem. Dumb idea."

"What's *our* idea?"

"After Kimberly died I assembled a team of drone technology experts—all outcasts—who cut their teeth with the top four U.S. companies. It took this group just nine months to create a miniature drone capable of firing a single shot with pin-point accuracy up to 100 yards while hovering in mid-air, or a quarter mile when perched on a stationary object like a rock or tree stump."

"How small is this aircraft?"

"About the size of one-and-a-half hummingbirds."

"I've never seen half a hummingbird."

"That may change, come lunch."

Callie frowns. "You're joking, right?"

"Let's just say Meat Stew covers a lot of ground."

She rolls her eyes and turns her attention to my work space. "I assume you can control your mini-drone remotely, with a laptop?"

"With a tablet, actually."

I activate my tablet, press a key to power the drone, press another to split the screen into four sections.

"What am I seeing?" Callie asks.

"The view from each camera."

"Where's the drone now?"

"Camp David."

"You flew it there undetected?"

"Pretty much. My flight range is only 30 miles, so I drove it to Smithsburg and launched it from there. It's got an infrared camera, so I was able to fly it into Camp David at night and perch it on the roof of the lodge building near the tee box."

"Why can't I see anything?"

"It's hiding in the V of the roof. If I lift the drone ten feet you'll be able to see the president and any guests he might have invited."

Callie looks at me with genuine warmth. "You've been planning this a long time," she says.

"I have."

"The president visited Camp David several times last month. You could have launched any of those times, but didn't. You saved this just for me."

"I don't know anyone on earth who'd enjoy it more."

"It's like old times."

"Yes. Except for—"

"Shh! Don't spoil it," she says. She leans over, kisses my cheek and whispers, "You're making me wet!"

"Uh..."

"Let's do it," she coos.

"Uh...just to clarify, you're talking about launching the drone, right?"

"Isn't that why you invited me to your extremely private work area where no one on earth could possibly see what we're about to do? Are you going to make me ask you formally? Fine, I will. Please, Donovan. Show me your mighty rocket. I want to see it rise straight up."

"Drone."

"That, too."

"You're too much." I slide my finger up the screen to raise the drone. When it's airborne, I adjust the long-range camera to offer a clear view of the president and two secret service men.

"That's amazing!" Callie says.

"Thanks."

"Think of the implications!"

I lower the drone onto the downslope of the roof, which offers a clear line-of-sight to the president, who's approximately 80 yards away.

"If you really want to get the president's attention—" Callie says.

"Yeah?"

"Kill his secret service guy."

"We're on *their* side, remember?"

"Right. I'm just saying—"

"—What, exactly?"

"Nothing says threat like a dead body."

"How about we just scare the shit out of him?"

She shrugs. "It's your party."

I study her a moment. "Are you okay?"

"Never better. You're right, by the way. You can't shoot the secret service guy. They'd think you were trying to shoot the president and missed."

I stare at her another moment, then remove an untraceable cell phone from my desk drawer and press the pre-programmed number. From the drone's camera we see one of the secret service guys checking his caller ID. He says something to the president, then answers the phone.

"Who is this?" he says.

I disguise my voice and say, "I'm running a test. I repeat, this is just a test. Tell the president to hold his scorecard high over his head."

The president asks who it is and the secret service guy says, "Sponge Bob." Before the president has time to look confused, the secret service guys are scanning the area with guns in hand. Then the first guy hands his phone to the president, who says, "Show yourself, Creed." Then he pauses and says, "Or Decker."

"Raise your golf card, Mr. President."

"Why?"

"Are you comfortable with the level of security at Camp David?"

He's clearly nervous, but says, "I am."

"Then raise your golf card over your head."

"What have you got in mind?"

"I want to see if I can read it."

"And if you can?"

"Then maybe you'll upgrade your security."

"I just did."

He's right. Suddenly, out of nowhere, six additional secret servicemen have surrounded the president and are moving him toward the lodge building. Keeping my voice disguised, I say, "I wouldn't enter that building if I were you."

It takes a second for the entire group to get the message. When they do, they push the president to the ground. Four men lie on top of him like human shields while the others stand, searching for signs of danger. While one guy calls for additional backup, the first one retrieves his phone and says, "What do you want?"

"Hold the president's scorecard over your head."

He reaches into the pile of people and eventually comes up with the scorecard, which he tentatively raises over his head. I shoot a hole through the center of it, and all hell breaks loose at Camp David. I end the call, and Callie and I look at each other and laugh hysterically, like high school kids who set off the fire alarm on the last day of school.

"What about the drone?" she says, between peals of laughter.

"It's programmed to return to the launch site at Smithsburg. It's on the way now."

"Turn on the camera so I can see it flying."

"I'd rather not transmit while the government's on high alert. If some teenager happens to find it they're liable to shoot him."

"See? This is why you get paid the big bucks. Worrying about some random teenager wouldn't have crossed my mind."

"Thanks. I think. Ready for lunch?"

"I'm not sure. What goes with hummingbird? Rooster knees?"

"Callie?"

"Yeah?"

"Be nice, okay?"

"I'm always nice."

I sigh.

She says, "You really want me to make an effort to be nice to Trudy?"

"I do."

"Then perhaps—just this once—you should let her sit at the grownups' table."

I sigh again, thinking: *This is going to be a long-ass lunch.*

Chapter 8

"SORRY I'M SMALL up top," Trudy said that first time, referring to her boobs. "You can see why I'm shy to show 'em."

"Don't be silly," I said. "They're perfect."

She laughed. "You're just horny."

True enough, but they *were* perfect in my view. I wanted to convince her, but fought the urge, figuring I'd gain more ground by reassuring her at a later date when she'd know I wasn't trying to get in her pants.

She said, "When I was ten my daddy told everyone my nipples were as tiny as tick turds."

"Your daddy's an asshole."

I wasn't just saying that. Her father *is* an asshole, and I can't wait to kill him. How bad is he? The bastard did jail time for molesting Trudy's sister, and although she hasn't said as much, I suspect he was inappropriately familiar with

Trudy, too. And don't even get me started on her brother! Far as I'm concerned, these two are dead men walking.

So...where was I?

Oh yeah. Our romance.

It took time for our romance to develop. We both had issues to overcome. Grieving over my daughter's death had been my full-time job. Not only that, but the scorched aftermath of my failed relationship with Callie convinced me that "happy ever after" might not be an option for a guy like me. Trudy had her own reasons for holding back, chief among them her concern that a contract killer might not represent the best possible role model for her child.

Not that Hawley is Trudy's birth child.

She isn't.

As I quickly learned, Trudy stole her from Rose Stout, who bought her from my former lover, Miranda Rodriguez. If you don't know much about me, I can see how this might be confusing as hell. But all you need to know is this: when I realized Hawley was my birth daughter, everything fell into place.

Eventually.

You've heard the old saying women need a *reason* to have sex, and men just need a *place*, right? Well, as you'd expect, I was ready to get physical with Trudy long before she was ready for me. After months of walks and dinners, I told her I was crazy about her. She held onto that information a few days before confessing she had strong feelings for me, as well. But she added, "Don't take that as a green light to wild monkey sex, 'cause I'll need to be kissed permanent first."

I didn't know what that meant, and told her so.

"It's a kiss that says our hearts are true, and our love's the permanent kind."

"You're putting a lot of pressure on our first kiss," I said.

"Your first kiss won't be the one that parts the curtains."

"Curtains?"

"Think about it."

I did. Then smiled and asked, "How many kisses would it take?"

"It ain't the number, it's the specialness. But don't worry. We'll know when it happens."

"Can you give me an idea what I'm looking for?"

"A kiss that says we go together like rama lama lama ka dinga de dinga dong."

"Excuse me?"

She laughed. "Never mind. Just kiss me."

I did. Several times. And continued kissing her for weeks. And one day she showed me her boobs. There was no buildup, it just happened.

As I admired the view she said, "It ain't an easy path."

"What ain't?"

"Lovin' a stone killer."

I smiled. "I don't kill stones."

"If only you did, it'd be so much easier."

"What if I stopped killing people?"

"I'd never ask a man to quit what he does for a livin'."

"Why not?"

"It's part of who he is."

"You don't think people can change?"

"*Men* people? Nope. And anyway, I don't like puttin' too many requirements on a man, 'cause those I'm drawn to ain't usually built for it. So I only have two. Wanna hear 'em?"

"Tell me the first one."

"Treat me right."

"That covers a lot of ground."

"Then you'll just have to cover it."

"I can do that. What's the second requirement?"

"Never cheat on me."

Before I could respond, she added, "Ever."

I said, "Luckily, I happen to be the most trustworthy man on earth."

"That's a mighty boastful claim."

"I'm willing to prove it, if given the chance. And just so you know, if my job ever starts coming between us, I'd stop."

"Killin' people?"

I nodded.

She frowned. "But you kill *bad* people, right?"

"Often."

"Then you're often doin' somethin' noble and good. Uh...have you killed women?"

I nodded.

"On purpose?"

"When I had to."

She took a deep breath. "*Children?*"

I nodded.

She said, "For money?"

"No."

"I don't understand. Are you sayin' they had it *comin'*?"

"They were casualties of armed engagements. What the government calls collateral damage."

"Like if you bombed a terrorist camp and a kid happened to be there you didn't know about?"

Experience has taught me it's best to answer some questions more vaguely than others. This was one of those times. "Yeah," I said. "Exactly like that."

"Then Donovan?"

"Yeah?"

"Don't *ever* promise to stop killin' people!"

I waited a moment to see if she was kidding.

She wasn't.

I looked at her curiously before saying, "Okay. But why?"

"It's bad luck."

"How so?"

"Tryin' to keep up with promises like not killin' people could get your loved ones killed. If Hawley's life was in danger and you had to kill someone to protect her I wouldn't want you hesitatin' on account of some stupid promise."

"Makes sense. How about you? Could you kill someone who threatened our kids?"

Her face broke into a giant smile. "Did you just say our *kids?* As in kids with an 's'?"

"Hypothetically."

"Anyone threatens our kids, I won't waste time hollerin' for you. I'll kill 'em myself. Are you ready for an important question?"

"Sure."

"Have you ever been unfaithful?"

"Only to girlfriends."

She shook her head. "You're about the sorriest husband prospect I ever met."

"Plus I'm twice your age."

"That part ain't an issue. My last boyfriend was your age, and I'd be with him still had he not accepted a blow job from a teenaged, suicidal ledge-walker."

"I have no idea what that means, but I feel comfortable saying that won't happen with me."

"You might be faithful if we were engaged or married, but I'd hate to be cheated on the whole time we're datin'."

"That wouldn't happen. You have my word."

"How can you make that promise? You barely know me."

"I know enough."

We were in my den the day she said, "Can we have a sip of the wine you poured last night at dinner?"

"Chateau Lynch-Bages? What's the occasion?"

"Pour it and see."

I did.

She took three long sips, then placed her glass on the table in the center of the room, slowly removed her blouse, and then her bra.

"Don't make too much out of this breast-barin'," she said. "This is just me, showin' good faith."

"Silly me for thinking you were proving the existence of God!"

"God don't need *my* help to be proved. But our special kiss does."

"The one that parts your curtains?"

"Yup."

I gave her the best kiss of my life and expected her to surrender faster than Dan Quayle's spell check program. A minute in I knew I was onto something, as she ripped the buttons off my shirt. I could tell she was waging a fierce war with herself to keep from going "all the way." She murmured, swooned, and when I kissed her neck and nibbled her ear she gasped and pulled me to the floor. "Oh, wow!" she said, over and over, her breath coming in spurts. I leaned on my elbow to survey my work and saw her face swaying gently from side to side, her lips slightly open, eyes half-closed.

"Mmm," she said, pulling my mouth back onto hers.

She kissed me like we were teenagers on a couch, TV in the background, and her favorite boy-band just won the People's Choice Award. I kissed her like I just heard the Patriots finally drafted an offensive line. But as my hand ventured closer to what she calls her "special place" she said, "Baby, I want you like Kirstie Alley wants Twinkies, but like Kirstie, we've got to stay strong and wait till it's right."

"It feels right to me!" I said, cheerfully.

She blinked twice, attempted to regain her composure, gave up and said, "I'll admit that was the best kiss I ever got."

"Really?"

"Yup. But it weren't the one."

"It—*What?*"

"Maybe we should try again."

I frowned, redoubled my effort, but...

"Nope," she said. "Maybe next time."

"Assuming I ever get past the curtains," I said, "where do they lead?"

She smiled. "So many ways to say it."

"Give me three."

"The Fun Zone?"

I laughed. "Cute. What else have you got?"

"Pink Portal?"

"Mmmm. Not bad."

"Kingdom of Labia?"

"Bingo!"

I thought I was right on the verge of entering said kingdom, since moments ago she was on me like rhymes on a rapper, but a full month passed before one of my random kisses made her say, "Omigod! That's the one!"

Go figure.

Chapter 9

THAT WAS THEN, this is now, and the three of us are sitting on the back patio, having lunch, when Callie says, "What do you guys do around here for fun? Besides whittling, I mean."

"We work out a lot," Trudy says.

Callie arches a brow. "He taught you how to fight?"

"He's workin' on it. We practice twice a day."

"Are you good yet?"

"You want to go a few rounds?"

Callie perks up.

"No she doesn't!" I say.

Callie says, "Sounds like I'm being challenged."

"You're not," I say, giving Trudy a warning look.

"We're the same size," Trudy says.

"She's right," Callie says.

"Stop it. Both of you."

"Yes, Daddy," Callie says, winking at Trudy, who's struggling to hold her temper. I give Callie my warning look and hope it takes.

She says, "I can tell you're athletic, Trudy. I'm sure you're a natural."

Trudy turns to me and says, "Be honest."

"About what?"

"How long would I last in a fight with Callie?"

I sigh.

Trudy says, "It's okay. I asked for your honest opinion. I can handle it."

"What kind of fight?"

"Hand-to-hand. No weapons."

"Are you asking how long it would take her to *kill* you? Or knock you out?"

"Knock me out."

I look at Callie. Then say, "It depends."

Trudy says, "Best guess."

"A serious fight?"

Trudy nods.

"Four seconds."

Trudy frowns. "I'm that bad?"

"No, of course not. But she's that good."

Callie tries to suppress a smug smile, but doesn't quite make it, which causes Trudy's eyes to smolder.

"Doesn't mean you're not above average," Callie says.

Trudy flashes a radiant, mock smile. "Why, *thank* you, Callie!" she says, her voice drenched with enough sarcasm to make Al Bundy blush. Then adds, "I'm sure Donovan could snap you like a twig."

Callie says, "It must give you a wonderful sense of security to feel that way about your man."

"Callie?" I say.

"Yeah?"

"Knock it off."

Callie's lips curl into a sly smile. "Would this be a good time to mention the gift I brought?"

Trudy looks at her with less anger, more curiosity.

"It's in my trunk," Callie says.

"You brought a *trunk*?"

"Yes, of course. Were you not aware Donovan invited me to stay for six weeks?" She laughs. "Look at your face! I'm kidding, Trudy. I wouldn't do that to you. The present—the main part—is in the trunk of my car."

Visibly relieved, Trudy says, "Is it something for the house?"

"Perhaps we should let Donovan decide. Now that I think about it, I should show it to him in private."

Trudy glares at her.

Callie says, "It's not personal, Trudy. I'm just not sure how much Donovan wants you to know about his life."

"I know a lot more than you think."

Callie looks at me. "Shall we test that theory?"

I shrug.

Callie says, "Are you aware your husband got his job with the government because he traffics in human suffering? That he—above all others in the nation—is considered the most capable of constructing terror scenarios designed to disrupt the economy, debilitate the national infrastructure, and destroy the very fabric of society? That he's our government's leading expert on torture? That he's highly capable of manipulating the public into hysteria, lawlessness, and civil disobedience? Are you aware that his daily thoughts are consumed by devising creative ways to commit mass murder of American citizens?"

Trudy waves off her comments with the flick of a wrist. "That's his day job, Callie. It's old news to me. And yes, I know he kills people for money. What else have you got?"

The look of surprise hangs on Callie's face several seconds. She looks at me as if waiting for me to stop her. When I don't, she turns back to Trudy, lowers her voice, and says, "Are you aware he keeps prisoners in the basement of this very house?"

"Of course. And by the way, we're down to just one prisoner."

"One?"

"He let Layla Hart go."

"That's the one who—wait. I don't know who that is."

"Layla was Kimberly's body double. Donovan hired her to pretend she was Kimberly. She'd meet him here, once a week, for dinner. It helped him get through a rough period."

Callie shows me a look that manages to incorporate both interest and horror. "You locked Layla in your basement and made her pretend to be your dead *daughter*?"

"I didn't intend to lock her up," I say, "but when she threatened to quit impersonating Kimberly I had no choice."

Callie turns to Trudy. "This is *acceptable* to you?"

"No, of course not. Layla was one of the first changes I made to the staff."

"Staff?"

"She was on the payroll, workin' on the premises, so I considered her staff. And anyway, Donovan took extra good care of her during her stay, and especially afterward."

Callie shakes her head in disbelief. "You might be crazier than he is. So who's left?"

"You mean in the basement? Faith Stallone."

"You know about Faith?"

"Of course. She and I have lunch on the patio from time to time."

"Isn't she in chains?"

"Not at lunch."

"What keeps her from trying to stab you with a fork?"

"Anson prepares her."

"What does *that* mean?"

"He gives her a mild sedative, ties her to the chair, stands guard."

"No straight jacket?"

"Nope."

"I think you're at risk."

I interrupt, saying, "Trudy's safe. Anson stands behind Faith with his gun loaded, cocked, and pressed to the back of her head."

"Well, *that* sounds normal. So tell me this, Trudy: Are you aware how Faith and Donovan met?"

"I'm a little sketchy on the hellos, but I know their first date involved fornicatin' in a men's toilet in downtown Cincinnati."

"Did he tell you he built a perfect replica of that men's room in his basement so he could relive the moment when serial fucking her?"

Trudy flashes me a look of disapproval before saying, "He sort of skipped over that part, but he did say their lovemakin' was always consensual."

"And you *believe* that?"

"Yes. And Faith confirmed it to me in person."

"Of *course* she did! She's his *captive*! What do you *expect* her to say? She's got a gun to her head. Literally!"

"Even so, I believe her. And besides, Donovan stopped fornicatin' with her when we became a couple."

"So far as you know."

"I'd know if it was otherwise."

"You're okay with Faith being locked up in the basement?"

Trudy shrugs. "It ain't the way I would have handled it, especially the part about recreatin' the men's room in the basement, but the way I see it, he showed restraint by not killin' her. I mean, Faith hired a hit man to kill Kimberly! Not only that, she's a witness to events that are better left untold. If Donovan were to set her free she'd tell those things to all the wrong people. So it was either kill Faith or lock her up. And Donovan was compassionate enough to give her a nice suite in his home to live out her days."

"Your attitude surprises me," Callie says. "In fact, it *shocks* me."

"Acceptin' things as they are ain't a big deal. It's just bein' practical."

Callie studies her a moment before saying, "You know a helluva lot. Far more than you should. Do you honestly believe you could walk out of here on a whim? Not to mention take the baby with you?"

"I know it for a fact, though it wouldn't be a whim. It'd have to be somethin' bad enough for Hawley to want to leave her birth father."

"If that's true, Faith isn't the only prisoner here."

"What do you mean?"

"You and the baby are holding Donovan prisoner."

Trudy shows her a severe look. "Even for you, that's a despicable thing to say."

"Is it? You've basically told me if he doesn't please you or the baby, you're both going to walk out on him."

"I expect every relationship on earth has that element. Some women are stuck in a bad marriage 'cause they can't afford to leave. Some are afraid to leave. Some don't want to put their children through a divorce. In a way I suppose *those* women are prisoners. But me and Hawley don't force Donovan to behave. We're just sayin' if he *don't*, we won't stay. I mean, would *you* stay with someone who abuses you or cheats on you?"

"I would not."

"He's a husband and father, and not our prisoner in any way. But for you to suggest he is, and the way you brought Hawley into it, was particularly ugly."

Callie says, "You don't like me, do you?"

"You're Donovan's closest friend."

"So?"

"I'll find a way to make it work."

"I seriously doubt you believe that. But whether you do or not, you should be completely honest with me."

"I'll always be honest with you."

"Then tell me how you feel about me at this very moment."

Trudy takes a deep breath, lets it out slowly, and says, "When I heard you were comin' I was overjoyed. Couldn't wait to meet you. And when I laid eyes on you I thought you were the most gorgeous, amazin', and coolest woman I ever met. I had the highest hopes we'd be close friends." Trudy looks away a moment, then sighs. "I truly did. But right away you started talkin' down to me."

"And how did *that* make you feel?"

"At first I thought you were just joshin'. You know, puttin' me through my paces and all, like a sister-in-law might do. But when I realized you were serious, my joy at havin' you here deteriorated faster than potato salad at a Fourth of July picnic."

Callie laughs. "And now that you know the *real* me how do you feel?"

Trudy sighs. "I fear you might be one of Satan's soldiers. But that don't mean I'm givin' up on us bein' friends."

Callie says, "I don't have any friends."

"One good one's all you need."

"I have very little to offer."

"Friendships don't have to start out fifty-fifty."

Callie thinks it over. "Would you expect me to apologize every time I fuck things up between us?"

"Yes."

Callie shakes her head. "It wouldn't work. I'm not a people-person. I'm rude, aggressive, and socially inept. I enjoy making people feel awkward. The nicer you treat me, the worse I'll be. You don't need proof of that. From the moment we met I've been deliberately baiting you, trying to make you angry."

"Why?"

Callie shrugs. "Who knows? I mean, I could obviously *manipulate* you better if I pretended to be nice, and Donovan's desperate for us to be friends, which could work to my advantage. But I'd rather push your buttons. It would be so easy to apologize and say I'm not usually like this, but this is exactly how I am."

"Why?"

"According to psychiatrists I'm an antisocial psychopath, with a malignant heart, capable of violent mood swings and aggressive social behavior. I lack empathy, and enjoy inflicting pain, both emotional and physical."

Trudy takes it all in, then smiles encouragingly. "I'm sure you have some wonderful qualities too, Callie."

Callie says, "Are you deaf or just fucking with me? Everything I just said: those *are* my best qualities."

Trudy—unsure how to respond—looks at me. I start to say something, but Callie's cell phone rings. She glances at the number, frowns. Accepts the call, asking, "Who is this?" Then, "How'd you get my number?" Then, "My *grandmother* told you to call?"

PART FIVE:
Sadie Sharp

Chapter 1

MOMENTS AGO, TALKING to Callie Carpenter's grand-mother, Sadie got an idea. It requires telling a lie, but since it's for the greater good—saving her own life—she just might be able to pull it off.

"My *grandmother* told you to call?" Callie repeats.

"Yes."

"Why?"

"I'm in trouble."

"I'm having lunch with friends. Can I call you back?"

"No offense, but can we talk now? It's pretty urgent."

"Make it quick. Where are you?"

"In your grandmother's room at Magic Manor."

"Why?"

"Two hours ago a man called and said he was going to kill me tonight."

"You've got my attention. Was this someone you know?"

"No."

"Go on."

"He said he'd let me live one more day if I killed your grandmother."

"He specifically referenced my *grandmother?*"

"Yes." Sadie winces at the lie.

"Hang on a minute."

Sadie hears Callie tell someone she needs to talk privately. Moments later she says, "The man told you to kill my grandmother, so you went to the nursing home?"

"I didn't know what else to do."

Callie pauses. "Are you mentally challenged?"

"Not the way you're implying."

"In that case I think you're the victim of an ugly prank."

"I don't think so. He killed Carol."

"Who's that?"

"My next-door-neighbor."

"When?"

"This morning."

"You saw Carol? You're certain she was dead?"

"Yes, absolutely."

"Do the police know?"

"I'm sure they do, by now."

Callie says, "If I run a background check on you, what am I likely to find?"

"Nothing bad."

"Ever been arrested?"

"No."

"Ever been admitted to a hospital or mental institution?"

"No."

"What's your legal name?"

"Sadie Lynne Sharp."

"If you're fucking with me you'll regret it."

"I wouldn't do that. Cecile already told me how dangerous you are."

"Exactly how did she phrase that?"

Sadie looks at Cecile before saying, "She said you killed your parents...and some other people."

Callie sighs. "Cecile has a big mouth, but we can deal with her later. In the meantime, start at the beginning. Tell me everything."

"When I woke up this morning I saw a note on my kitchen counter that said 'Tonight You Die.' At first I thought it might be my husband, playing a joke. So I called him at work, but he didn't know anything about it. Then we thought the person who wrote the note might be in the house, so I ran to my neighbor's, but—"

"She was dead."

"Right. And minutes later the guy who killed her called my cell phone and told me to kill your grandmother."

"Did he say 'Kill Callie Carpenter's grandmother' or did he give you her name and location?"

"Name and location."

"And you told Cecile all this and she gave you my number and said I could help?"

"Yes."

"And you're with her now?"

"I am. Would you like to speak to her?"

"No."

"What should I do, Ms. Carpenter?"

"If I were you I'd kill Cecile."

"*Excuse me?*"

"It's a no-brainer: Cecile wants to die and you get an extra day."

Sadie shakes her head in disbelief. "If I kill Cecile will you still help me?"

"I wasn't going to help you in the first place."

"Why not?"

"You're dealing with a serial killer who chose you as his victim."

"So?"

"You should be grateful."

"*Grateful?*"

"He likes you. Probably plans to perform all sorts of sexual perversions before, during, and after your death."

"*After?*"

"It's fairly typical."

"I don't want him to perform perversions on me at *all!* At *any* time! Much less *kill* me."

"Have you thought to tell him that?"

Sadie frowns. "Of course!"

"And that didn't discourage him?"

"It didn't appear to."

"Then I'd say you've got a serious problem."

Sadie looks at Cecile in frustration. Cecile responds by lifting her finger to the side of her head and making circles, indicating her granddaughter's crazy.

No shit! Sadie mouths. Then, to Callie, says, "Would *you* be able to kill him?"

Callie laughs.

Sadie says, "This is *funny* to you?"

"You may as well ask if I can fry an egg."

"How much would I have to pay you?"

"To fry an egg?"

"To kill this asshole."

Callie chuckles. "Every time I start to hang up on you, you say something interesting."

"I wish I could return the compliment," Sadie says.

Callie pauses a moment, then laughs. "You've got balls."

"I most certainly do *not*...unless you're implying I'm forthright in my speech. I hear *that* a lot and it usually means I've said something offensive. If so, you shouldn't take it personally. I'm terrible with people and even worse at conversing with strangers. But getting back to the issue at hand, how much would I have to pay you to remove this man from my life?"

"What's it worth to you?"

Sadie thinks a moment. "Eighteen thousand dollars."

Callie laughs. "That's all your life is worth?"

"Any more than that and I'd have to go in debt."

"Then go into debt."

"I'd rather die."

Callie laughs again. "You sound more fucked-up than me. What do you look like?"

"Excuse me?"

"How hot are you?"

"Right now or when I'm fixed up?"

"Right now."

"Amanda Bynes."

"Bullshit."

"Okay, so I was exaggerating. But I'm nice-looking. A solid eight on the ten-scale is what my husband's friends say."

"Prove it. Take a selfie with my grandmother and send it to me."

"Why?"

"I might be willing to work with you."

"I don't understand."

"Think about it."

"You mean sex?"

"Sex and eighteen grand."

"I'm not into women."

"I sure hope not! That's what makes it interesting."

"I don't believe in cheating on my husband."

"Even better. Adds an element of taboo."

"I wouldn't know what to do with a woman."

"You'll figure it out. Tell me about your boobs. Real or fake?"

"Does it matter?"

"Not really."

Sadie pauses. "Real. But just to be clear, I won't have unprotected sex with a stranger."

"Fine. I'll bring a gun."

Sadie sighs.

"You're interrupting my lunch," Callie says. "You want my help or not?"

"Hold on. I'll take the picture."

She does; then sends it.

Callie says, "Granny looks happy."

"She *is* happy. She wants to die." Sadie hesitates, then says, "So what do you think? About me?"

"You mean do you look good enough for me to take the job? Yes. What do you say?"

"Am I supposed to be grateful you're willing to rape me?"

"What do *you* think?"

Sadie waits a long moment before saying, "Thank you."

"You're welcome. And by the way, it's not rape when both participants consent...even if one of them screams while it's happening."

Sadie's eyes grow large. "Are you planning to hurt me?"

"I won't rule it out."

"How long a session am I agreeing to?"

"*Session?* Jesus. How about we play it by ear."

"I'd rather have something in writing."

"No you wouldn't. Because that would piss me off."

Sadie sighs. "What happens next?"

"I don't suppose you happen to have the killer's phone number?"

"I do, actually."

"Okay, good. Cecile has a cell phone the orderlies are supposed to charge every week. If they haven't, and the battery's dead, you'll want to charge it and text the killer so he'll know you switched phones. In the meantime, kill Cecile, avoid the police, and wait for the killer to call you. When he does, tell him you'll do whatever he wants if it'll buy you extra days."

"How do I avoid the police?"

"Start by removing the battery from your cell phone so they can't track you."

"I've got a new phone."

"So?"

"It requires tools to remove the battery."

"Then smash it and throw it down a sewer drain. But first, ask Cecile if she knows her phone number."

"You don't have it?"

"No. Does that surprise you?"

"I suppose not."

As it turns out, Cecile can't remember her own phone number, but says her phone's in the top drawer of her night stand. Sadie finds it, checks the power.

"It's more than fifty percent charged!"

"Lucky you," Callie says. "Are her car keys in the drawer?"

"Yes."

"Call me from Cecile's phone."

Sadie does. Callie says, "Okay, got her number programmed in my phone. Did you drive to the nursing home?"

"No. I walked."

"Anyone see you?"

"Probably. But no one I know."

"Good. Are you familiar with Brightwood Shopping Center?"

"It's about two miles from here."

"Cecile has a car in the storage facility a block or two past the center. I don't know the address, but she'll have it written down somewhere. Here's the plan: kill Cecile, take her phone, destroy yours, get her car, drive somewhere safe, then call me."

"Okay."

"Sadie?"

"Yeah?"

"Say nothing to your husband."

"Why not?"

"He might be involved. And most importantly—"

"Yes?"

"Bring your checkbook."

"I-uh…"

"Let me guess: you don't have it."

"No, I do. But…how could you cash a check without being implicated?"

"I do this for a living, remember?"

Sadie debates asking her next question, but can't help it. "Is eighteen thousand dollars really that important to you?"

"It buys your commitment."

"I'm totally committed already. My life is on the line."

"And your body."

"Isn't that enough?"

"No."

Sadie sighs. "Who do I…I mean, to *whom* do I make the check?"

"Don't write it till I tell you. And when you do, it'll be to yourself."

"Why?"

"I only deal in cash."

"And flesh, apparently," Sadie says. "You want the killer's phone number?"

"Why?"

"In case he kills me before you get to him?"

Callie says nothing.

Sadie says, "I just want to make sure my money isn't wasted. If I'm paying you to kill a man, I want him to die whether he kills me or not."

Callie laughs. "I like you. Go ahead. Text it."

Sadie does. Then says, "I guess it's time. Any last words for your grandmother?"

"Tell her I'll see her in hell."

Chapter 2

FOR SOMEONE WHO claimed she wanted to die, Cecile put up a hell of a fight. It took five minutes and every ounce of strength Sadie could muster to put the old girl down. With that finally done, she left Cecile's room undetected, got all the way down the hall only to realize she left the murder weapon—the pillow—in Cecile's room. She raced back, got the pillow, decided to take it with her, then changed her mind, started heading back to her mom's room, changed her mind again, spun around, and took it with her out the front door.

The storage unit took longer to locate than she expected, and the combination lock required twelve attempts to open. But open it she finally did, only to find the car battery just as dead as its original owner. So Sadie retraced her steps to Brightwood Shopping Center, bought and carried a new battery all the way back to the storage facility, where twenty minutes of labor convinced her how hard it was to remove corroded battery cables without tools, and how easy it was to get covered in grease while trying to do so. She cursed, walked back to the shopping center, purchased some pliers and a screwdriver, and finally replaced the battery. To Sadie's extreme relief, the car started right up.

Now, driving out of the storage facility's parking lot, the killer calls.

"Where are you?"

"Fleeing the scene."

"You killed someone?"

"Yes. Can I call you back? I'm trying to get away without getting caught."

"Are you walking or driving?"

"Driving."

"In whose car?"

"The victim's."

"I'm impressed. Drive to Charlottesville. When you get there, give me a call."

"Why?"

"So I can tell you where to pick up the key."

"The key to what?"

"Your hotel room."

"You booked a room in my name?"

"What do *you* think?"

"I think you used a fake name. What is it?"

"I'll tell you when you get to Charlottesville."

Sadie pauses. "Are you planning to be there?"

"No. And don't worry, I'm not coming for you. Unless you lied about your kill."

"I never lie." She pauses. "Well, hardly ever."

"But you *did* kill someone."

"Yes."

"I assume you have proof?"

"Two photos. Before and after."

"Send them."

"I'm driving."

"Then find a place to park. I'd like to see them immediately."

"Fine."

"The victim: man or woman?"

"Woman."

"Was it your mother?"

"Certainly not!"

"Let me guess: Magic Manor old folks' home?"

Sadie pauses. "How did you know?"

"Do I really need to say it? You're predictable. I simply asked myself the same question I asked you: where does a person such as yourself find a victim on short notice? It would have to be nearby, free from prying eyes, and the victim would have to be easy to kill. First thought? Relatives. Second? Friends. 'Does Sadie have any relatives in town?' I asked myself. Then I remembered your mother resides in a nursing home just blocks from your house. Wouldn't she be an easy mark? Or maybe she could point you to one of the terminal residents. If someone was about to die anyway it wouldn't weigh so much on your conscience to perform a mercy killing."

"You really expected me to kill someone at Magic Manor?"

"Yes. Or a friend or homeless person. But how'd you know this woman had a car?"

"I beat it out of her."

He laughs. "You got lucky with the car. She volunteered the information. Gave you her phone and car keys hoping you wouldn't kill her."

"Something like that."

"You killed her with your bare hands?"

"No. I used a pillow."

"You sure she's dead?"

"Of course."

"It's not easy to smother someone to death with a pillow."

"No *shit?* Thanks for the update."

"I haven't received the pictures yet."

"I haven't sent them."

"Why not?"

"I just this second got off the expressway. Traffic's backed up. I'm on the ramp. When the light changes, I'll find a place to park."

"Why didn't you just strangle her with your hands? Wait. Don't tell me. I know."

"I doubt that. Okay, the light's changed, traffic's moving."

"You didn't want the old lady looking at you while you were killing her. Am I right?"

"Probably. Whatever. Can I ask you a question?"

"Go ahead."

"How come Rick never called me back? Why didn't the police or 911 show up at Carol's?"

"Rick never made the call."

"What do you mean?"

"Rick has a reserved parking space at his office, behind the building."

"So?"

"He exited the building, but never made it to his car."

Sadie screams, slams on the brakes, swerves into the parking lot of a sandwich shop. She pulls to a stop and says, "What do you mean he never made it? Is he—?"

"Relax. He's not dead, just drugged. But he *will* be dead if you don't do exactly as you're told."

"We had a deal."

"We still do."

"Our deal was me killing someone and getting a full day to live. There was nothing about having to save Rick's life."

"You *don't* have to save his life. I just assumed you'd *want* to."

"Rick's on his own."

"That seems harsh."

"Where was he when I needed him? He couldn't even manage to call 911 without getting kidnapped."

"Fine. Don't save Rick. Do you want a second day?"

"Not if I have to kill someone else."

"You won't."

"Then what?"

"I'll tell you when you get to Charlottesville. In the meantime, send me the photos."

He hangs up.

She sends the photos, then gets back on the expressway, points Cecile's car toward Charlottesville, and calls Callie Carpenter.

Chapter 3

"GRANNY'S DEAD?"

"Yes."

"You got her car?"

"I'm driving it now."

"And the killer?"

"I just spoke to him. He booked me a room in Charlottesville, Virginia. Said he'll tell me which hotel when I get there, and where to find the room key."

"Did he say whose name is on the registration?"

"No."

"Shit. Has he said what you have to do next?"

"He'll tell me when I get there."

"Is he at the hotel now? Or planning to meet you there?"

"He said no. But this just in: he kidnapped my stupid husband in broad daylight, coming out of his office building."

143

"How'd he manage that?"

"Probably lured him into a panel truck with the promise of magic beans."

"The good news is your husband doesn't seem to be involved."

"I already knew that."

"The bad news is the killer might be leading you into a deadly ambush."

"You think I should drive somewhere else? He doesn't know what car I'm in."

"If he told you to kill my grandmother, he certainly knows about her car. Trust me, if he wants to kill you, he'll find you. Did he threaten to kill your husband?"

"Yes."

"Then you should continue on, to Charlottesville."

"Will you come?"

"I suppose I *have* to."

"What do you mean?"

"If we're going to have sex before he kills you, I'd better head there now."

"Kill him first, okay?"

"Sorry. Pleasure before business. No exceptions."

"I'm tired. Exhausted."

"No problem. I'll do all the work."

"I'm covered in grease."

"I'll bathe you."

Sadie takes a deep breath to keep the anger from her voice. "My mind won't be in the game. I'm upset about my husband. And even if I knew he was safe, I'm worried for my life. I'd be the worst lover imaginable."

"I'll keep my expectations low. But Sadie?"

"Yeah?"

"This is going to happen. Today, within the next two hours. Do you understand?"

When Sadie fails to respond, Callie says, "Tell me you understand."

Sadie stares through the windshield a moment, watches the city gradually turn to countryside. Then says, "You'd do this to me with the full knowledge it's something I'm dreading?"

"Yes."

"You don't care how I feel about it?"

"Not really."

"Great. And having sex with me against my will is the only way you'll kill the man who burst into my life out of nowhere, kidnapped my husband, and threatened to *kill* us?"

"Yeah, that's right. Sex and eighteen thousand dollars."

While Sadie quietly fumes in her car, Callie takes her own deep breath and says, "I'm not the monster you're making me out to be. You asked for *my* help, remember? Just to be clear, I charge fifty grand to kill an average person. Plus expenses. You want your husband dead? Fine. Give me a fifty grand, I'll take care of it. On *my* timetable. But the guy *you* want me to kill is no average person. He's a stone killer, who at the very least has broken into two homes undetected and killed your neighbor. Well guess what: that's a *million-dollar* hit. I don't know you from Adam, except that you chose to kill my grandmother to save your own life, and now you expect me to perform a million-dollar hit on *your* timetable—which is immediately—and all you're offering is eighteen grand and the promise of lousy *sex*?"

"Well…"

"Yes Sadie, I'm expecting the sex because it was part of our deal. You think I'd kill your husband and let you stiff me for half my fee?"

"No."

"Well, eighteen grand is the smallest amount I've ever accepted, and even though the sex can't be worth more than a few hundred, it's still half my fee."

"I understand that, but—"

"We had a deal, Sadie, a sacred contract. I'll advise you to be very careful about weaseling out of it, unless you're prepared to have your arms hacked off your torso."

"I—*Oh, God!* Um…you're right, of course. About everything….I'm…so sorry. I'll try my best to be…um…a good…lover."

"Don't let me drive all the way to Charlottesville to get stood up."

"I won't."

"Say it."

"I won't stand you up."

"I'm not overstating when I say your life depends on keeping me happy."

"I know."

"Then how about showing some fucking gratitude?"

"I…yes. I'll try. I mean…I will. I promise."

"All I'm asking."

They're quiet till Callie says, "How long before you get there?"

"Forty-five minutes."

"I'll actually arrive before you. So call me before you call the killer. I'll park somewhere and tell you where to drive. When you pass me, I'll fall in behind and make sure he's not following you."

"Thank you Callie!"

"My pleasure."

PART SIX:
Callie Carpenter

Chapter 1

Three hours earlier...

AFTER ENDING THE first call with Sadie, Callie made her way back to Creed's patio, where she found the two love-birds grinning at each other like they'd just invented sex. Though happy for Creed, it was enough to make her gag. He looked up when she entered.

"Everything all right?"

"Yeah, but I gotta run. I know that breaks your heart, Trudy."

Creed said, "You mentioned your grandmother."

"I did?"

"On the phone, a few minutes ago."

"Right. Someone called to give me some news about her."

"I was under the impression your grandmother died years ago."

"Yes."

"Did she?"

"No. But I did give you that impression."

"So she's alive?"

"Not any more. She passed."

"When?"

"Just now."

Trudy jumped to her feet, came around the table, arms outstretched, saying, "Oh, Callie! I'm so *sorry!*"

Callie could see she was, but had no use for the impending hug. "Stop!" she commanded.

Trudy did.

By then, Creed was on his feet. "How can we help?" he said.

"There's nothing you can do. But thanks for offering. It's not a big job, just a few arrangements to make." She looked at Trudy and felt compelled to say, "Thanks for lunch. What *was* that dessert, by the way? The flavor was astonishing."

"Persimmon puddin'."

"*Seriously?*"

Trudy nodded.

"I've never tasted anything like it."

"Donovan's gonna let me plant some persimmon trees."

"You can't just buy them in...uh...some sort of store?"

"We could, but they're hard to find around here. And anyway, I like growin' 'em, 'cause I can tell what kind of winter we're gonna have by lookin' inside the seeds. But you probably already knew that about persimmons."

"Shockingly, no."

"Really? Well, the inside of each seed grows a design that resembles a knife, fork, or spoon. Spoon means we're gonna have a real bad winter, with heavy snow that sticks. A fork means a mild winter, with snow that don't stick to the ground."

"And the knife?"

"That's a freezin' cold winter, with winds that'll cut through you like a sharp knife."

Callie looked at her long enough to make sure she wasn't joking, then said, "At any rate, Donovan was right: you're an excellent cook. And thanks for making the effort just now, but I don't need to be comforted. My grandmother had cancer. She was old, dying, and in a lot of pain. You'd probably call her death a blessing." She paused a moment, then added, "Before you ask, there won't be a funeral."

"*What? Why not?*"

"I didn't like my grandmother, and she didn't like me."

"I'm sure she loved you very much, Callie. She probably just didn't know how to show it."

"She was certainly good at showing hatred. When I was a kid she prayed every night that I'd suffer a horrible death." She glanced at the floor a minute, then back at Trudy, and said, "But we're past that now. As for you and Donovan being married? I was confused at first, but like you said, I want what's best for him. If that's you and the baby, then I'm happy for you both. That said, no offense, but I don't want to be your friend." Trudy started to speak, but Callie waved her off. "I know you mean well, Trudy, but I'm a lost cause. I don't like getting close to people. I always disappoint them, or they disappoint me, and when it's all said and done I wind up having to kill them."

Trudy removed a thick, four-inch wide metal bracelet from her wrist, and handed it to Callie. "I know this ain't your style of fashion, but it'd please me no end if you'd accept this bracelet as a gift."

Callie said, "That's very nice of you, but—"

"I'll make you a deal. Put it on now and don't take it off before midnight, even if you're in the bath or shower. Do that, and I'll stop pushin' to be friends."

"You promise?"

Trudy puts her hand up. "I do."

"What happens at midnight?"

"You'll have good luck."

Callie laughed. "Good luck when the clock strikes twelve?"

"I'm not sayin' exactly *when* the good luck'll happen. But it always happens by midnight of the first day."

"I don't believe in charms, Trudy."

"No one does, till they work. Please. Put it on right now and wear it till midnight. If nothin' good happens you'll be able to prove me wrong. At midnight you can give it to someone, or throw it away."

"I may not be interested in friendship, Trudy, but I would never throw your bracelet away."

"It won't matter if you do, 'cause whether you keep it, give it, lend it, lose it, hide it, toss it, or throw it away, it always finds its way back to me."

Callie smiled. "I bet I could keep it from coming back to you."

Trudy smiled back. "You know what I always say?"

"What's that?"

"Prove it."

Callie sighed, put on the bracelet, and stared at it. "Maybe I'll buy a lottery ticket."

"Maybe you should."

Callie looked at Creed. "Have *you* worn it?"

He laughed. "She hasn't trusted me with it yet."

"Your wrist's too big," Trudy said. "And anyway, you don't need good luck. You've got me and Hawley."

As if on cue, the baby started hissing. Trudy cocked her head to listen.

Callie said, "Is that normal?"

"No," Creed said, rushing toward her. "What's wrong, Trudy?"

"Nothin'. She's fine. Just chattin', and such."

"I think she might be having a seizure," Callie said.

"I promise she's okay."

"She's hissing louder."

"It's okay. Are you drivin' east?"

Callie nodded.

"Then you've picked a good time to be on the highway."

"Why's that?"

"Snakes."

"I'm sorry. Did you say snakes?"

"Yup."

"How many?"

"Lots."

"When?"

"Directly."

"Let's see if I've got this right: the baby starts hissing, and right away you assume it's a sign that snakes are about to descend on the property via the highway?"

Trudy laughs. "Not just the highway. Best I can tell, they're comin' from everywhere."

"I'll make you a deal, Trudy. I'll wear the bracelet till midnight if you'll see a shrink."

"If that's what it takes, I'll be glad to. But it won't be today."

"Why not?"

"'Cause we're about to get busier than jumper cables at a redneck weddin'."

Callie looked at Creed and said, "You poor thing." Then, rolling her eyes, she said, "Guess I'd better hit the highway before the snakes show up. Sorry to cut the visit short. I had fun shooting at the president with you."

"Me too," Creed said.

"If you'll give me a second to grab my stuff, you...and Trudy...can follow me to my car and decide what you want to do about Megan."

"Who's Megan?"

"Megan Fry. She's one-half of the present I brought you."

"I don't understand."

"Can we speak freely?"

He glanced at Trudy, then nodded.

Callie said, "Megan Fry is Faith Stallone's identical twin sister." She grins. "I can tell by the look on your face I finally told you something you didn't know. Well, good for me, I've earned my keep."

"You're certain about this?"

"Do you really need to ask?"

"No. Sorry. Fill me in."

"Last year when Kimberly was diagnosed brain dead, I wanted to know who made the diagnosis, and why her condition deteriorated so quickly. You'd have done the same had you not been so close to the situation. When Kimberly died, you sort of withdrew into your fortress here, so I tracked down key members of the hospital staff and persuaded them to tell me who evaluated her, and who diagnosed her as brain dead. And you know who they said? Megan Fry."

"*What?*"

"Megan was a brain specialist for the Academy of Neurology. She's the outside expert the hospital contacted to check Kimberly's brain function during her coma."

Trudy said, "That don't sound like a coincidence to me."

"Nor to me," Callie said. "And a small amount of prodding got Megan to confess who hired her to kill Kimberly."

"Faith Stallone?"

"Nope. Believe it or not, it was our good friend Ryan Decker."

Creed's face does a slow burn. "How?"

"He gave her a contact poison to rub between Kimberly's toes."

"You're certain it was Decker?"

"Positive. But since Megan's in the trunk you can ask her yourself, in your own way."

"I really don't know what to say, but...thank you...for doing this."

"You're quite welcome. But there's more. Give me a sec, okay?"

She left the room for a minute and returned carrying a three-ring binder, which she placed in Creed's hands.

"What's this?"

"The second part of my gift. As you know, Faith won the Powerball lottery but never got a chance to collect the proceeds. But I bet you didn't know Megan found the ticket and collected the money."

As Creed shook his head in disbelief, Callie said, "You'll be pleased to know I confiscated most of the winnings from Megan's account, just over $46 million, and used it to fund a trust in Kimberly's name to provide college scholarships for deserving youth."

"Omigod!" Trudy said. "That's *amazing*! *Say* something, Donovan!"

"I don't know what to say. Thank you, Callie. This really touches my heart."

Callie said, "The binder contains all the paperwork pertaining to the trust. You'll see it's currently managed by one of the top attorneys in Louisville, but you have total control and can make any changes you like."

Creed thumbed through the binder. "This must have taken you months to put together."

Callie smiled. "It did. But the look on your face is worth it."

Minutes later, when Callie popped the trunk of her car open, Trudy said, "If that's Megan, I think she's dead."

"Just heavily sedated," Callie said. "As the outside air hits her she'll—"

As if on cue, Megan's arm started twitching. Creed looked at Trudy and said, "Can we keep her?"

Chapter 2

NOW, IN CHARLOTTESVILLE, Callie pulls into a Waffle House parking lot and waits for Sadie's call. When it comes, she says, "Turn right on Exit 120, drive approximately two miles, then turn left on 250. When you see the Medical Center, pull into the parking area, park your car, and wait to hear from me."

"Where will you be?" ·

"You're not supposed to know. If you see me, I've failed you."

"What if the killer calls?"

"Ignore him. And don't call him back till I say it's okay."

"Will you be able to recognize my car?"

"*Your* car?" Callie laughs. "So much for Granny. But yes, I'll know it when I see it. Now hang up and wait for my call."

Twelve minutes later Sadie's phone rings.

Callie says, "The good news is you weren't followed."

"You're sure?"

"Positive."

"How do you know he isn't watching from a distance?"

"Because this is what I do. Now lower both windows on the driver's side, and turn off your engine."

"Lower them how far?"

"All the way."

"Okay. Windows are down. Engine's off."

"Good. Now set the volume on your phone as loud as it'll go, and put it on speaker. Then hang up, call the killer, and talk exactly the way you've spoken to him in the past. If he asks where you are, tell him."

Sadie adjusts her phone as directed, then places the call. When the killer answers, she says, "I'm here. In Charlottesville."

"Where exactly?"

Sadie swallows hard and says, "At the Medical Center."

"You're parked?"

"Yes."

"Prove it. Text me a photo of the front of the building."

"I'll have to step out of the car."

"Then do so."

Sadie exits the car, snaps the photo, sends it. Then climbs back in the car.

A moment later he says, "Thanks for being honest. That means a lot. Do you know where Cherry Park is?"

"No."

He tells her, then says, "There's a bench in the park near the corner of Cherry and Ridge Streets. Sit there and wait."

"For what?"

"Within five to twenty minutes a woman will sit beside you, holding a plastic grocery bag. Don't say a word, just wait for her to leave the bag. Inside you'll find a wig, sunglasses, change of clothes, ball cap, and the key to Room 216 at the Fontaine Hotel. There's a restroom near the bench where you can change into the wig and clothes. Then go to the hotel and call me from the room."

Sadie says, "Why do I need to wear all that stuff?"

"The police have probably found Carol's body by now, and Rick's employer might be wondering what happened to him. If they check around they'll learn you're missing too, and you're pretty enough that the media might take up your cause. That's how it works, you know."

"How what works?"

"You can tell how pretty a girl is by how hard the media covers her disappearance."

"I doubt that's true."

"Pretty faces, hot bodies: that's what the public wants to see. Want an example? What's that girl's name, the one who was kidnapped from her home as a kid and got rescued nine months later?"

"Elizabeth Smart?"

"That's right. Can you name any other kidnap victims?"

"They found three teenage girls living in a house last year. One had a baby."

"That's right. Can you name them?"

"No."

"Each year more than 30,000 kids are abducted in America and the only one you can name is the pretty one, years ago. Speaking of which, I bet you remember the young blonde that went missing in Aruba."

"Natalee Holloway?"

"Bingo. Did you know the guy accused of killing her admitted to killing another girl years later?"

"Of course. He's in prison. What's your point?"

"Do you remember *her* name?"

She thinks a minute, then says, "No."

"She wasn't as photogenic as Natalee, so she didn't get the same press coverage. Do you remember the pretty young girl accused of murdering her roommate in Italy a few years ago?"

"Amanda Knox?"

"That's right. Can you name any other female murderers?"

"Not off-hand."

"Each year thousands of women commit murder. But the one you remember happens to be gorgeous. See my point?"

"Whatever. Fine, I'll wear the wig. But you lied to me."

"When?"

"You promised I'd be safe tonight."

"I promised not to *kill* you tonight. And I won't."

"Maybe not, but when I go to the park you'll know exactly where I am, and what I'll be wearing."

"So?"

"I don't think that's fair."

He laughs. "That's funny. I like you, Sadie. And that's a good thing."

"Yippee," she says, sarcastically. "What do I have to do next?"

"I'll tell you when you get to the room."

"Are you going to be there?"

"No. And like I already told you, I'm not coming. Not tonight, anyway. You have my word."

"I'm supposed to trust you?"

"You can." He pauses. "I don't know what else to say. I already gave you my word."

"You did. Thank you."

"Remember not to speak to the bag lady."

"Okay."

They hang up. Sadie sits quietly a moment, turns her head to look out the window, and screams.

"Relax," Callie says.

"Omigod! You're...her?"

"If you mean Callie, yes. Nice to meet you."

"You're...gorgeous!"

"If I am, it's not by choice, believe me."

"How'd you get that close to me? I didn't hear a sound."

"That's me, doing my job." Callie rounds the car, hops into the passenger seat, says, "I heard the whole conversation."

"How's that possible? Where were you?"

"Under the car. And I've got some bad news for you."

"If you're about to tell me I'm burning oil, I already knew that."

Callie gives her a funny look. Then says, "I'm serious, Sadie. This is *really* bad news."

"*Really* bad? Wow, there's a shock. Let's see if I've got this straight: in the space of six hours my life's been threatened, my neighbor murdered, my husband kidnapped, I've been forced to kill an innocent woman, flee the city, pay a hit woman eighteen thousand dollars to rape me. If you've got some *really* bad news I guess you may as well just say it."

"I think I know who the killer is. I recognize his voice."

Chapter 3

"YOU—SERIOUSLY? BUT...that's *good* news, isn't it?" Sadie says. "I mean, why *wouldn't* it be good news?"

"Because if the killer's who I think he is, he's a major player."

"By major you mean—Wait. Are you backing out of our deal?"

"No. But I thought you should know what we're up against."

"This guy. Can you kill him?"

"Yes. Unless he knows I'm involved."

"He knows you?"

"We're elite contract killers. It's a fairly small community. What I'm wondering, why send *him?* You're easy enough to kill....Unless...."

"Unless what?"

"Shit."

"What's wrong?"

"This isn't about you."

"What do you mean?"

"He's coming for me."

"*What?*"

"He gave you the name of a specific person to kill at Magic Manor: a woman who happened to be my grandmother. Until now I assumed no one knew Cecile and I were connected, and it was pure coincidence she tipped you off about me. But as I said earlier, Granny had a big mouth. Now I realize they were probably in collusion."

"Who?"

"The killer and Granny."

"Uh...Callie?"

"That's the only logical explanation. The killer set this whole thing up with Granny. Probably promised he'd get a nice young lady—you—to put her out of her misery. In return, she'd help him set me up by giving you my name and number. After all these years, wouldn't my bitchy grandmother love to be the one who fucked me and set me up to die?"

"I think you're reading way too much into this."

"I don't think so. It makes perfect sense. It changes everything."

Sadie sighs. "There's something I need to tell you. Please don't be angry."

Some part of Sadie's brain registers the razor-sharp knife pressing against her throat, but it got there so quickly she hasn't had time to process it. She's aware Callie's looking around, making sure no one's sneaking up on her, hears her say, "Is this an ambush? Did you set me up?"

As her predicament becomes clear, Sadie whispers, "Please don't kill me!"

Convinced she's safe—at least for the moment—Callie says, "What have you done? Why are you afraid I'll be angry?"

"It's not a huge deal, I don't think. I mean, this isn't about you."

"I'm listening."

"Can you remove the knife from my throat, please?"

"I can, but I won't."

Sadie swallows carefully. "Remember the first time we spoke, and I said the killer told me to kill Cecile?"

"Yeah?"

"That was a lie."

"He *didn't* tell you to kill Cecile?"

"No. He just said I had to kill someone before five o'clock. It could be anyone."

"How did my grandmother make the top of your list?"

"Magic Manor's close to my house. My mother's a resident there. I knew they had several terminal residents, and figured if I *had* to kill someone it would be more humane if—"

"Don't lie to me!"

"I'm not!"

"You really expect me to believe you chose my grandmother because it's more humane to kill a dying woman?"

"Yes," Sadie says. She pauses. "I mean, I *did* expect you to believe that."

Callie sighs. "I really want to like you, Sadie, but you're making it difficult."

"How can I make things better between us?"

"Be honest with me in all things. Being a killer myself, I know exactly why you chose Cecile. But I want to hear you say it."

"Can you lower the knife first?"

"No. I can't abide liars. I'm barely in this with you right now."

"Okay. The real reason I picked Cecile is because I knew it would be easier to kill an old, dying woman than a young, healthy man."

"And you picked Magic Manor because?"

"I knew they were understaffed. I doubted anyone would check on the terminal patients because no one wants to be the first to discover a corpse."

"Anything else?"

"I really *did* consider it less of a crime to kill a dying person, and I was glad to learn Cecile wanted to die. But...you're right. I was looking for the easiest murder I could commit and get away with. I'm sorry I tried to dress it up by lying."

"I forgive you," Callie says. She kisses Sadie's lips, then lowers the knife. "I'm surprised you didn't think about killing a baby."

"I considered it. But where am I going to find an unguarded baby on short notice?"

Callie laughs.

Sadie says, "Are you angry?"

"More relieved than angry."

"You're *that* afraid of the killer?"

"No. But I'd be a fool not to be concerned if he's been plotting to kill me for a period of time."

"How good a hit man is he?"

"If he's who I think he is, he's damn good. Which still begs the question: why send *him* to kill *you?* Is there something about you I should know?"

"I don't think so. I mean, I'm just a housewife."

"They don't send this guy to kill housewives. Are you related to a Senator or some other type of career criminal?"

"No."

"Billionaire? Industrialist?"

"No, nothing like that. I'm just a regular person, with regular friends and relatives."

"Well, if that's true...I have another theory."

"What?"

"I'll tell you after we make love." She strokes Sadie's thigh.

Sadie looks around. "You don't mean right *now*, do you? Don't we have to find the park and get the clothes and hotel key first?"

"We do. We'll take separate cars. Granny didn't have GPS, but I do. I'll drive there first, check out the drop area, then call and give you directions."

"Will you be watching me in the park?"

"Every moment."

"Thank you."

"I'm just protecting my investment."

Chapter 4

"THE WIG LOOKS stupid," Callie says, dumping the contents of the bag onto the sink. "And the clothes? Moronic."

They're in the ladies' room at Cherry Park, a mere sixty yards from the drop point where Sadie met the bag lady minutes ago. Callie picks up the wig and works her fingers through the skull cap.

"What are you doing?"

"Searching for the transmitter."

"Surely you don't think the killer would—"

"Ah! Found it. Tell me I'm good!"

Sadie shrugs. "This is insane. Total overkill. I'm a housewife."

Callie removes a pocket knife from her handbag and digs the transmitter out of the netting. "Here," she says. "Put it in your purse. When you get to your room, leave your purse there and come find me."

"Where will *you* be?"

"In the connecting room next to yours, if it's available."

"And if it isn't?"

"I'll make the occupants an offer they can't refuse." She notes Sadie's expression and says, "What's wrong?"

"I sort of figured you'd be staying with me through the night. You know, in case he comes for me."

"He promised he wouldn't."

"And you *believe* him?"

"Not really."

"I have a feeling he's coming tonight."

"We can only hope, but I doubt we'll get that lucky."

"Can you stay in *my* room, just in case?"

"No. We can't let him know I'm helping you."

"How would he find out?"

"He's had access to your hotel room."

"So?"

"It only takes minutes to install miniature video cameras."

Sadie's face suddenly contorts. "*What?* That's so *gross!* It's...Omigod, it's disgusting!" She thinks a minute, then says, "Even in the *bathroom?*"

"Of course. Why not?"

"Oh...my...*God!*"

"I could locate and remove them, but not without being seen. Not to mention that doing so would *really* get his attention."

Sadie shakes her head. "This is unacceptable. I can't function under these circumstances. I'll have to insist on spending the night with you, in your room."

Callie laughs. "You're offering me a *sleepover?*" Her eyes make a thorough sweep of Sadie's body, and settle on her backside. "I accept. I could really get into that!"

Sadie turns her body enough to hide the view. "You don't mean...uh...*literally*, do you?"

Callie tosses her head. "I won't rule it out." She goes outside to stand guard while Sadie changes. When Sadie exits the bathroom wearing the clothes, wig, and sunglasses, Callie bursts out laughing.

Sadie frowns. "It can't be *that* funny."

"Oh, but it is! You look like...oh, God, I can't even come up with what you look like! A whorehouse drag queen? No, wait! I've got it: you look like Natasha, from Rocky and Bullwinkle!"

"Oh, great."

"Hey, Rocky, watch me pull a rabbit out of my hat!"

"Hilarious."

"Nuthin' up my sleeve!"

"Got any more?"

"Oops! Wrong hat! Say it."

"What?"

"What Natasha says: 'Hello, dollink!'"

Sadie shakes her head. "Who'd have guessed this is what it's like to spend an afternoon in the park with a hit woman?"

"No doubt about it," Callie says. "I've gotta get a new hat!"

Chapter 5

"WHAT CAUSED THIS?" Callie says, tracing a small scar on Sadie's breast.

"My doctor found a lump. It turned out to be benign, but the surgery left a scar."

"They did a good job. It's hardly noticeable."

"I have others. Sorry."

"We all have scars. Mental and physical. Don't worry, I'll find all of yours by the time we're done." She kisses the scar, and slides further down Sadie's body.

Sadie says, "I wish you'd let me shower first."

"You're fine. I like you this way. Now tell *me...*if *you...*like *this!*"

Sadie gasps.

She *does* like it, but dares not admit it.

Twenty minutes later, after her third orgasm, Sadie's phone rings.

"It's him," she says. "What should I do?"

"Put your phone on speaker and take the call."

She does, and the killer says, "What's going on, Sadie?"

"What do you mean?"

"You were supposed to call me when you got to your room. By my count you're an hour late."

"I didn't think you meant to call you immediately. I thought I had the night off."

"I'm not sure where you got *that* idea, but shake it off, because I've got a task for you."

"When?"

"Tonight, starting at ten."

"*Starting* at ten? How long is this going to take?"

"I'm not sure. There are a number of variables, so plan on being available for the duration."

"What do I have to do?"

"It's not *that* big a deal. I mean, it's something you've probably done a hundred times before. Even so, I doubt you're going to be happy about it."

"*There's* a shock. How about you just tell me?"

"Very well. You're having sex tonight, in your hotel room."

"*What?* No way!"

"Sorry, but this is non-negotiable."

"Bullshit! And while we're on the subject of my hotel room—" The look on Callie's face tells her to shut up immediately, so she does. But the killer says, "What about your hotel room? Is there a problem?"

"No. It's just that you said you weren't coming here. In fact, you *promised*! And now you expect me to give you *sex*? Unacceptable! It wasn't part of the bargain."

"Relax, Sadie. I'm not the lucky guy."

"Excuse me?"

"I'm not the one coming over."

"You pimped me out to some *stranger?*"

"Yeah."

"You *bastard!*"

He sighs. "Let's move along shall we? The guy's name is—well, you can call him Joey. He's been told you're a hooker, paid in advance by his cousin to make sure Joey has a good time. If he *does* have a good time, and if you can keep him in your room for at least an hour, I'll add a week to your lifespan."

"A full month. Nothing less."

"You're in no position to bargain."

"Yes I am. It's one thing to let a guy fuck me. Quite another to make sure he has a good time."

Callie smiles, shows her a thumbs-up.

The killer pauses a long time before saying, "You make a good case. You're right, there's a difference between just lying there and giving your best effort. That said, I don't need him to fall in love with you, just to stay in your room for an hour. Bottom line, a month is out of the question. But I'll give you two weeks."

Sadie looks at Callie.

Callie nods.

The killer says, "But if you think we're establishing a precedent for you to haggle with me in the future, you're going to be seriously disappointed. As for tonight, don't let me down, Sadie. If you do, all bets are off, and this will be your last night alive. Understood?"

"Yes."

Sadie ends the call and looks at Callie. "What's our plan?"

"You'll need to go through with it."

"*What?* You expect me to fuck *Joey?* I thought you were going to *protect* me!"

"I will. We've got adjoining rooms. We'll unlock the connecting doors. I'll be a few steps away the whole time. You'll be safe."

"It won't work. If there are cameras in the room, and you run in to protect me, the killer will see you and know you're helping me."

"If things get to that point, it won't matter."

"I've got a better idea."

Callie laughs. "This should be interesting."

"What if I wait in your room until he knocks on the other door? I can poke my head out and tell him I've switched rooms. When he comes in, you can smack him in the head and knock him out."

"Just like that?"

"That should be simple for someone with your experience."

"It *would* be, if we wanted to royally screw the pooch."

"I have no idea what that means."

"Figure of speech."

"If it is, it's the worst one I've ever heard. What does it mean?"

"It means the killer has a plan. He wants Joey to have sex with a hooker."

"The killer said to keep Joey in the room for at least an hour. Who says he has to be conscious the whole time?"

"The killer did, when he told you to have sex with Joey, and show him a good time."

"What difference does it make if Joey has a good time or not?"

"It makes all the difference in the world to the killer."

"Why?"

"Remember a couple hours ago when I said I had another theory why someone might hire this particular killer for this type of job?"

"Yeah, so what?"

"The conversation you just had with him supports the theory."

"Which is what?"

"He's using you...and Joey...to achieve something much bigger than it seems."

"I'm exhausted, Callie. Can you say that in plain English?"

"I think there's something much bigger going on here than a guy threatening you, kidnapping your husband, killing your neighbor, forcing you to kill a random person this morning, and making you fuck Joey tonight."

"Like what?"

"I'm not sure, but it's all coming together at ten p.m. Everything he's forced you to do has been leading up to this one key moment. I think the critical element of the killer's plan is to distract Joey with a hooker while he does something that will take him an hour to do."

"Like what?"

"I don't know. But it's not going to end well for Joey."

"I don't give a shit about Joey."

"Nor does the killer, I expect. But the bottom line is you're buying the killer enough time to do whatever he needs to set Joey up. And if Joey thinks anything's going on other than having a pleasant hour or two with a hooker, the killer's plan turns to shit. And if that happens, he's already warned you: all bets are off."

"You honestly expect me to fuck this total *stranger?* A guy who sleeps with *hookers?* Joey's probably got a thousand diseases!"

"The answer's yes. I expect you to fuck Joey....Unless I can figure out the killer's plan."

"Is that possible?"

"Eventually, yes. By ten tonight? No, probably not. But I'm going to try."

"How?"

"Same as always: shake some bushes, make some calls."

"Can I stay here while you do that?"

"No."

"Why not?"

"My calls are private. And anyway, you'll need to shower and get all dolled up for Joey."

"I can shower in your room. If the water's running I won't be able to hear your conversations."

"Sorry."

"Look, I don't want the killer spying on me, okay? It's creepy as hell. Nor do I want videos of my naked body plastered all over the Internet."

"This guy couldn't care less about seeing you naked. The only reason he's got cameras running—if he does—is to make sure his plan goes smoothly."

"You say that with confidence, but just admitted you have no idea what his plan is."

"Not yet, but I'll work on it the minute you leave. Which needs to be now."

"I *really* don't want to be naked in my room."

"And I *really* don't want you here while I'm making calls. So you're just going to have to suck it up, Sadie."

"Easy for you to say."

Callie arches an eyebrow. "Are we about to have...a situation?"

Sadie sets her jaw. "I guess not...*bitch!*"

"Well, that's lovely. Thank you for that."

"Fuck you."

"We already did that, Sadie, and you were exactly as advertised: lousy in bed."

"That's a *lie!* You *loved* it."

Callie glares at her a moment, then softens a bit. "You're right. I did love it."

"I'll do it again if you let me stay. And better, I promise."

They stare at each other in silence. Sadie says, "Please?"

Callie stares a bit longer, then says, "Have you ever whored?"

"Of *course* not!"

"Then...okay."

"Okay what?"

"You can stay."

"Omigod! *Seriously?*"

"Yes."

"Say it again."

"You can stay."

"What about tonight?"

"What about it?"

"I don't want to be naked in that room *ever!* And I don't want to have sex with a total stranger."

"You won't have to."

"But you said—"

"Forget what I said. I'm going to take your place."

"*What?*"

"I'll go to your room tonight. I'll fuck Joey."

Sadie frowns. "You're joking. It's not funny, Callie."

"I'm dead serious."

Sadie searches her face. "You'd do that for me?"

"Yeah. I would."

"Why?"

Callie laughs. "I have no fucking idea!" Then she says, "Well, that's not true. Like the killer said, there are lots of variables. Whatever his big plan is, it appears to be totally dependent on you pleasing this guy. And I don't think you have it in you to come through. At the last minute you'll either back out or make a mess of it."

"You're right. If I had to go in there and have sex with a total stranger, I'd screw the pooch."

"That's not quite how the expression works."

"I don't care! The minute I left your room I was planning to get in the car and drive till I ran out of gas."

"Stupid plan. You'd be dead before you got to the first town."

"You're giving him way too much credit. He couldn't possibly find me that quickly."

"Of course he would! You think he's operating *alone*? Remember the bag lady at the park?"

"*She's* working with him?"

"No. Or he wouldn't have told you not to speak to her. But I guarantee he had someone watching you while someone else put a tracking device on your car."

Sadie, overwhelmed, says, "If that's true, no matter how good you are, you might be in over your head. You're just one person, and now you're telling me this guy—who was already extremely dangerous on his own—has *associates?*"

"I wouldn't be surprised."

"Then we should get the fuck out of here! We should get in your car and drive somewhere safe."

"It doesn't work like that. There *is* no safe place. He'll kill your husband, then you. Then me, if he can."

"Callie? I don't want you having sex with this Joey character. It's not right, and something really bad might happen to you."

"I've whored before," Callie says. "I'll be fine."

"You know what else we could do? We could ignore Joey. Stand him up and wait for the killer to come after me. When he does, you could hide in the room and ambush him."

Callie laughs. "Your plans always involve hiding in the room and smacking someone over the head!" She laughs again. "This isn't a TV show, Sadie."

"Fine," Sadie sniffs. "So how does it work in real life?"

"If one of us doesn't fuck Joey tonight the killer won't come to the room to hunt you down. He'll blow up the hotel."

"That's crazy."

"It's what I'd do."

"You people are *insane!* Uh...no offense." She sighs. "I hate to even bring this up, but you can't take my place. If there are cameras in my room, the killer will see you, and know you're helping me."

"After hearing his last conversation, I doubt he'll care. In fact, he'll probably be relieved it's me instead of you."

"But won't he kill me for backing out?"

"I don't think so. In fact, I doubt he ever planned to kill you, assuming you came through for him with Joey."

"If it's not about me, why kill Carol? Why kidnap Rick? Why make me kill someone? Why not just hire a local hooker to keep Joey happy?"

"Good question. Wish I had the answer. He chose you for a reason. I'm not sure what it *was*, but he clearly felt he could control you. Or at least manipulate you. Maybe I'll ask him after I smack him over the head and knock him out."

Sadie sighs. "You're sure you want to do this?"

"Of *course* I don't! But I don't want to see *you* get hurt, either. Because if you've never whored before you have no idea how hard it is to fake interest, or how quickly things can get out of hand."

"You think Joey's dangerous?"

"Let's just say I doubt he's some random john looking to get laid. He's a major player of some sort, and the killer's throwing you in his path because you're expendable. It's no skin off *his* back if Joey kills you, as long as you keep him occupied for an hour."

Sadie stares into Callie's eyes and holds her gaze. "If you're truly serious about taking my place tonight, I'll never be able to find words strong enough to express my gratitude. I'll owe you for the rest of my life."

"Super. That covers me for two weeks, anyway."

"I *mean* it, Callie. Who in the world would do something like this for me? There's no way I could ever repay you."

"I disagree."

"What do you mean?"

"Take off your clothes and we'll think of something."

"I'm serious, Callie."

"Me too."

Sadie shakes her head. "You have a one-track mind."

"You might be right. Take off your clothes and let's find out!"

"I will if you will."

As they undress, Sadie says, "This time I'm going to be the best lover you ever had."

"You think?"

"I swear!"

"That's pretty big talk, coming from a straight, married woman."

"I'll prove it. You'll see."

Chapter 6

AFTER GIVING CALLIE the best sex of her life, they order room service. Sadie turns on the TV and says, "Omigod! What's going on?"

Callie glances at the screen. "Turn it up!"

Sadie does, in time to hear a news reporter say:

> "We're coming to you live, from Bedford County, Virginia, where snakes are terrifying local residents as they appear to be emerging from hibernation all at once. In the past hour, thousands have been sighted on roads, highways, farms, and yards. This unprecedented activity for the species is confounding experts, as the snakes appear to be moving in concert.

> "The following video, taken moments ago by local residents Carla and Glen Suggs, shows what

appear to be more than sixty snakes crossing their patio from north-east to south-west. According to city officials in Roanoke, the snakes are mostly garter and water snakes, but nearly all of the roughly thirty-five snake species in Virginia have been spotted, including the three venomous ones indigenous to the state. Area residents are cautioned to keep a safe distance."

She pauses, glances at a note and adds, *"Those three venomous snakes include the Eastern Cottonmouth, the Northern Copperhead, and the Timber Rattlesnake, whose bite is considered lethal.*

"The Richmond Herpetological Institute is urging people not to confront the snakes. They say while not aggressive by nature, 80% of all snakebites occur when people attempt to capture or kill them."

The camera cuts to Glen, who says, *"I never saw anything like it. They're moving across the yard like a brigade of soldiers. They're as organized as a school of fish."*

Carla says, *"What's that? Naw, they don't scare me. I've been married twice."* She looks at Glen. *"No offense, honey."*

The camera cuts back to the announcer who says, *"What you're seeing on your screens is not a hoax or trick photography. It's a live video feed from our News 8* camera crew that documents the movement of hundreds of snakes, in all varieties, as they move across city streets, heading in the same direction, north-east to south-west, as if migrating. To where, you ask? 'Too soon to tell,' says Vlad Dubuque, research zoologist, U.S. Department of Vertebrate Zoology."

The camera cuts to Vlad, who says, "It's highly unusual for snakes to be visible in these numbers. Obviously, the recent rains and floods are a factor, and we can't rule out the polar vortex. But the idea that these snakes are all migrating, or heading to a specific location is preposterous."

The camera cuts back to the announcer. "Preposterous or not, this reptilian activity has not been limited to the local area. Calls are pouring in from counties throughout south-western Virginia. In Carroll County, snakes appear to be traveling north. In Wythe, east. In Bland, south-east.

"Despite what experts have said, Dr. Avery Woolworth, professor of mathematics at UVA, has plotted a rough course of progression based on the reports, and believes the snakes are set to converge in a single location at approximately ten p.m., a densely-wooded area located some fifty to eighty miles south-west of Bedford, Virginia. In the meantime, the Virginia and West Virginia highway departments have urged all residents within 100-miles of Roanoke to stay inside, remain calm, and limit all driving *activity to emergency situations until further notice. State police say if you must drive, exercise extreme caution. We now return you to your regularly-scheduled programming, but will continue to monitor and update the situation as further developments occur."*

"That's terrifying!" Sadie says. "You think it's the End of Days?"

"No. But I *do* think Hawley's mom has got it going on."

"What do you mean?"

"I'm not really sure."

Room service arrives. The ladies enjoy a light dinner, then Callie gives Sadie her car keys and says to drive somewhere close by, but safe, like a restaurant, and wait for her call.

"It's only nine-thirty," Sadie says.

"Better to leave too early than too late."

When they hug goodbye, Sadie experiences an overwhelming sense of dread. She remains in the hall till she hears Callie's shower running, then takes the elevator to the ground floor and exits through the back entrance. When she finds Callie's car she drives to the nearest busy restaurant, a place called Orange Park Café, and pulls into the parking lot. Though it's dark, she sees a well-built guy coming out the front door, heading to his car....

...And gets an idea.

Chapter 7

WHEN CALLIE OPENS the door, Joey nearly faints. "I was looking for Sadie."

"I'm Sadie. Please, come in."

He does, but says, "This can't be right. You look way better than your photo."

"Thank you."

With a puzzled expression on his face, Joey opens his phone and shows her a picture of Sadie. Callie says, "I have a confession to make. I'm not the Sadie your cousin booked. She wasn't feeling well, so I stepped in to take her place. I hope you're not disappointed."

"No, not at all!" he says, enthusiastically. "In fact, I'm delighted."

"I'm so relieved to hear that!"

"What's your name?"

"Sadie."

"I mean your real name."

"Callie."

"Well Callie, you're the most beautiful woman I've ever seen!"

"What a lovely thing to say!"

Callie's phone rings. She glances at the caller ID and says, "Please forgive me, Joey. I need to take this. Make yourself comfortable. Have a drink."

He checks his watch. "I'm on a strict timetable."

"I'll make it worth your while," she coos. "I promise."

He smiles, and Callie accepts the call: "Hi Donovan."

"Hi yourself."

"How's Megan?"

"As well as can be expected. It's a big adjustment for her, but she's settling in. You know what she told me?"

"I couldn't guess."

"She said you've been holding her in the basement of a farmhouse for nearly a year."

"She's a whiner. Has she seen Faith yet?"

"No, but Trudy wants me to invite them for dinner tomorrow."

"Bless her pea-pickin' heart."

He laughs. "You really should give her a chance."

"You keep trying that on, but it never fits."

They're quiet till he says, "You busy?"

She glances at Joey, who's chugging a mini bottle of vodka, while mentally undressing her.

"Kinda," she says.

"Quick question?"

"Sure."

"Do you have any idea how many people live in Virginia?"

"Not off-hand."

"Eight million, two hundred and sixty thousand."

"You knew that or looked it up?"

"I looked it up just now."

"Why?"

"I wanted to know what the odds were that the random person Sadie Sharp chose to kill on an hour's notice happened to be your grandmother?"

"Sounds like fate to me."

"Callie?"

"Yeah?"

"What the fuck are you doing?"

"I could ask you the same question."

"Why are you helping Sadie? Is this about your grandmother?"

"No. It's about protecting her. From you, as it turns out."

"She has no money. She can't pay you."

"I know."

"You gave her your car, told her to drive somewhere while you take her place with Joey."

"Is that a problem?"

"No, but your car was at my place all morning."

"So?"

"My guys tricked it out."

"Then they must have informed you Megan was in the trunk."

"They did, but I told them to leave her there. I knew you'd get around to telling me how a carbon copy of Faith Stallone happened to be in your trunk, unconscious."

"And now you know."

"How many cameras have you spotted?"

"Three. How many are there?"

"Three. I see you've met Joey."

"Yup."

"He looks eager."

"Positively. It could've been you, you know."

"We tried that, remember?" He sighs again. "You shouldn't be there. You've insinuated yourself in the middle of a dangerous operation."

"That's your fault. We're a team. You should've asked for my help."

"I didn't want to put you at risk. If this goes sideways, it needs to fall on me alone."

"Well, I'm in it now, so you may as well spill it."

"How much do you know?"

"Almost nothing."

"There's no time to fill you in right now. But since you've chosen to be there, I need you to keep Joey busy for at least an hour."

"That shouldn't be a problem."

"Don't let him leave till I call you back."

"Okay."

"Callie?"

"Yeah?"

"Be careful. I'm watching, but if something goes wrong, I'm still thirty minutes away."

"Even with the snakes?"

He chuckles. "Whatever else you think about Trudy, you have to admit she called it. But yeah, I can be there in thirty. I've got a chopper, and last I checked, snakes can't fly. Be careful with this guy. Stay focused."

"Okay."

"And whatever you do..."

"Yeah?"

"Don't let him handcuff you."

"Got it. Thanks for calling. Bye."

She hangs up, turns to face Joey, flashes a perfect smile. "Sorry for the interruption, handsome. But from here on out...I'm all yours!"

He smiles broadly and says, "You like it rough?"

She cocks her head. "Rough is good. Within reason."

"Perhaps we should choose a safe word, in case I go too far. Any suggestions?"

Callie looks into the camera and says, "How about *persimmon*?"

Joey shrugs, reaches into his bag. "I was told I could handcuff you to the bed."

"That's news to me," Callie says. "But if it makes you happy, I'm game."

As he approaches, she says, "Those look real."

Chapter 8

"SHOULDN'T I TAKE my clothes off first?" Callie says, eyeing the handcuffs.

"No. This is better. It fits the fantasy."

One glance at the headboard tells her why Creed reserved this particular room for Sadie: the headboard is oak, with a thick center post that appears to have been manufactured for the sole purpose of securing a set of handcuffs. "Are you sure you want to use those?" Callie purrs. "I'm very skilled with my hands."

"I'm sure."

"Perhaps if you explained your fantasy I could make it even better than you imagined."

"That won't be necessary. Please, extend your wrists."

Callie does so, and Joey cuffs her with one set of cuffs, then attaches another set to the bedpost, and leans in to connect the cuffs together. Callie still has time to totally incapacitate him. It's either strike now, or be completely at his mercy.

She allows him to secure the cuffs.

He takes a few steps back to admire his work. Then says, "You are truly a gift from Allah. I'm blessed."

"Thank you."

"Do you know what an altar is, Callie?" Before she has time to respond, he says, "An altar is any structure upon which offerings are made for religious purposes. Tonight your body will be my altar."

"It's flattering to be worshipped."

"Not worshipped. Sacrificed."

"Excuse me?"

"This is a special night, Callie."

"For you and me?"

"Yes. But especially for the movement."

"I don't understand."

"Nor do you need to. You only need to do two things: fulfill my sickest, darkest, most twisted sexual fantasies, and pay for my sins with your blood."

"You're planning to cut me up?"

"I'm planning to kill you."

"Why?"

"It's how we're celebrating my last night on earth."

"I don't think so, asshole."

Joey's in the earliest stage of being startled, but never gets to experience the full effect, as Callie's perfect kick makes contact with the side of his head. He flies backward, unconscious, and lands on the floor at the foot of the bed. Callie frowns, looks at the speaker and says, "What now?"

There's a small hiss as the sound system activates under the bed. Creed says, "I told you not to let him cuff you."

"Sue me."

"I just hope to hell you didn't kill him."

"I couldn't have. I purposely missed his temple."

"I saw that. But you kicked him full force."

"I only had the one shot, so I took it. Anyway, he's not dead. I can hear him wheezing."

"Good."

"Can you send someone to get these cuffs off?"

"Sorry. Can't let Joey suspect we're on to him. But I'll send Ben Terry to your room to remove whatever weapons Joey brought."

"Won't *that* tip him off?"

"Maybe not. He's pretty groggy."

"You expect me to lie here and wait for him to wake up?"

"I do. Hopefully Joey will wake up, fuck you, and be on his way."

"What if, after fucking me, he tries to beat me to death with a lamp or chair?"

"Or iron."

"Excuse me?"

"There's an iron in the closet."

"Perfect way to die. Imagine the irony."

"If he tries to kill you, feel free to kick the shit out of him."

"How long will it take Ben to get here?"

"Ten minutes, give or take."

They're interrupted by a noise that sounds like someone's trying to break into one of the hotel rooms. Not Callie's but close by. Then the door to the connecting room opens, and a wiry, amped-up hillbilly says, "Well, looky here!" He grins. "You never know what's goin' on behind closed doors. I sure hope I ain't late for the party!"

Chapter 9

CALLIE LOOKS AT the camera, rolls her eyes. Creed remains quiet. The hillbilly takes a minute to survey the situation and says, "Got any drugs?"

"Nope," Callie says.

"Booze?"

"Sorry. What brings you here?"

He points his thumb behind him, indicating the room he just broke into. Says, "First room off the elevator on the second floor. Connectin' door was open." He looks at Joey's body. "What happened to your boyfriend?"

"He passed out."

"Are you really handcuffed, Sweet Thing, or just fakin'?"

"I'm really handcuffed."

"You mean I could just waltz on over and cop myself a feel?"

"I don't think so."

"Why's that?"

"You don't look like much of a dancer to me."

He stares at her blankly and takes a knee. Callie can't see what he's doing, but hears him roll Joey over. "This man's been clobbered," he says. "You done that?"

She hears him going through Joey's pockets.

"Great golden gobs of goose shit!" he hollers. "I come to steal a car and this sumbitch's got five thousand bucks cash!" He stands and stuffs the wad of cash in his pocket. "Was this meant for *you*, Sweet Thing?"

Callie says nothing.

"I reckon it *was*, pretty as *you* are." He glances at Joey and says, "Who the hell pays five grand for pussy? Ain't there no barnyards in Charlottesville?" He fixes his eyes on Callie's crotch. "Nothin' personal, Sweet Thing, but I gotta see it for myself."

"Just like that?" she says.

"What do you mean?"

"What about that whole middle part, where you wrestle with your conscience and come to the conclusion it's not appropriate to molest a helpless woman?"

"There's only two things I need to think about."

"What's that?"

"You got a five thousand dollar pussy, and I want to see it."

As he starts to approach her, she makes an athletic move to adjust her posture.

He says, "You're wound up tighter than a coiled rattler. Relax, Sweet Thing. I'll probably just kiss and pet it some." As he reaches for her crotch she explodes into action. Kicks his arm aside with one foot and scissors the other into his side hard enough to break two ribs.

He screams, falls backward into the wall, hits hard, slides to the floor, sits there, grimacing.

"*Shit!*" he howls. "Holy, fuckin' *shit!*"

He rolls onto his good side and gasps, "I think you broke my fuckin' *arm!* And I *know* you done broke my *ribs.*" He wipes tears from his eyes and says, "Am I *cryin'?* Holy shit!"

He rises to a sitting position, shakes the cobwebs from his brain. "I ain't been kicked that hard since I took a shine to my billy goat." He staggers to his feet and says, "But it takes a lot to discourage *me,* Sweet Thing. In other words, I *did* fuck the billy goat."

Callie says nothing, content to plan her next assault.

As the hillbilly stumbles toward her, Joey starts coughing.

The hillbilly spins around.

Callie says, "Maybe you should just fuck *him.*"

Joey *wants* to sit up, *tries* to sit up, but falls back down. The hillbilly stands over him, ready to strike, but notices Joey's bag on the chair. He goes through it, says, "Holy shit!"

Now he's holding a 9mm Walther PPS in his good hand, another set of handcuffs in the other. Before he thinks to threaten Callie with the gun she says, "Why do you need a car?"

"Huh?"

"Why do you need a car?"

"My truck's impounded. I need wheels, man."

"Where you headed?"

For a split second, he looks at her in a non-sexual way. "Are you from around here, Sweet Thing?"

"Not really."

"You know anyone locally?"

"I know a few people. Why?"

"I'm searchin' for my wife, Trudy Lake. She done run off with some rich motherfucker from outside Roanoke name of Donovan Creed. You ever hear of him?"

Forty possible responses go through Callie's brain before she chooses: "What makes you think he's from around here?"

"I got a P.I. to run a search on my Trudy Jean. Turns out she done *married* the sumbitch. Marriage license was filed at the circuit court of Roanoke, Commonwealth Virginia. Home address turned out to be some attorney's office. You think that makes the marriage illegal?"

"No." Callie says, then laughs. "Did you say her middle name is *Jean?*"

"Naw, that's just what I call her. On account of that Monkees song where they say 'Cheer up Sleepy Jean?'"

"Trudy suffers from depression?"

"Oh, *hell* no! In fact, she's one a' them"—he tries to make finger quotes, but his arm won't work—"eternal optimist types. But that don't mean I never came home to find her in a foul mood, bein' I'm a drinker, and she don't tolerate abuse."

"She hits back?"

He grins. "Let's just say she's been known to come at me multiple times with a Barlow knife, and not just when I was conscious. But I love her despite all that and her other shit. So anyway, if this Creed fella lived in Richmond, he wouldn't apply for a marriage license in Roanoke, would he?"

"I suppose not."

"I imagine he'd have to live within fifty miles of Roanoke, though that covers a lot of ground. I aimed to drive around, ask people if they knew him, but like I say, they impounded my truck."

"How'd you get to Charlottesville?"

"Hitched a ride with some yokel."

"Why didn't you steal *his* car?"

"I planned to, but I passed out durin' the ride. When I come to I found myself on the edge of town in an empty, broken car. So I'm gonna steal *your* car—or your boyfriend's—and go find that sumbitch Donovan Creed and take back what's mine."

"Your ex-wife?"

Darrell scowls. "Trudy ain't my ex. You think I give a shit what them papers say? When she stood before the Lord and made her vow you know what she said?"

"I must've been out of my mind?"

"Nope."

"Oh my God I've made a terrible mistake?"

"Nope. She said, 'Till death do us part.' Do I look dead to you, Sweet Thing?"

"Not yet, but you're getting close."

He bursts into laughter. "Oh, Lord, but I love it when a pretty girl talks trash." He laughs again, then points the gun at Callie, cocks the hammer, and grins. "You got anything else to say, Sweet Thing?"

"I guess not."

"In that case I reckon we can proceed to the fuckin' stage of our relationship."

Chapter 10

"THAT DOESN'T MEAN what you think," Callie says.

"What don't?"

"That business about cocking the hammer before pulling the trigger. I know they do it in the movies, to enhance the suspense and let the popcorn eaters know the gun's ready to fire. But cocking the hammer doesn't make the gun any more ready to shoot than it already was. It just wastes two seconds of time you could've spent shooting me."

"That's bullshit. You cock the hammer, then pull the trigger."

"You can if you're stupid. But just so you know, pulling the trigger cocks the hammer *for* you."

"You're tryin' to trick me."

"Whatever," Callie sighs. "You know what? Just shoot me."

"What?"

"You've only got two choices here, Gomer: either kill me, or learn where Trudy is. But sex is out of the question, because I'll tell you right now you're not going to touch me. And if you think your *ribs* hurt, imagine what I'll do to your dick if you come within three feet of me."

He rubs his chin. "I *will* imagine what you could do to my dick, Sweet Thing, though I reckon I'll call bullshit on you knowin' Trudy's whereabouts."

"Why's that?"

"'Cause that'd be one hellacious coincidence."

"In that case I've got a question for you."

"Let's hear it."

"When's the last time you tasted Trudy's persimmon pudding...Darrell?"

"What the *fuck*? You know my *name*?"

"Either that or we've experienced one hellacious coincidence."

"Where's Trudy?"

"With Donovan Creed. Wait. What time is it?"

He checks his watch. "Ten twenty-two. Why?"

"She's probably blowing him right now."

He scowls. "You got a mouth on you, Sweet Thing. Maybe I'll give you a chance to see what a *real* blow job looks like."

"Go ahead. Joey's still unconscious, he won't complain. Just drag him where I can watch when you go down on him."

"You know what you are?" he snarls. "A smart ass."

"It's not my fault. I tried to be a dumb ass, but everyone kept calling me Darrell."

"Fuck you!"

"Sorry. Not gonna happen."

"Where's Trudy?"

"In the arms of another man."

Joey starts coming to.

Darrell grits his teeth, walks over to Joey, puts the gun to his head. "Tell me right now, or I'll kill your boyfriend."

Callie laughs. "You think I give a shit if you kill him? You already stole my five grand."

Darrell curses in frustration and bolts across the room, staying well clear of Callie's legs. When he gets to the wall, he follows it to the bed, grabs his gun by the barrel, and swings it hard against the side of Callie's head. Except that her head is no longer where it was when he began the attack. She's bent her knees and lifted her body two feet higher. While the gun misses her head, it hits her rock-hard midsection flush. Fortunately for Callie, the force of the blow is greatly diminished because she was already allowing herself to fall back to the bed at the moment of impact. As that's happening, she launches her left knee and strikes Darrell's bad arm hard enough to break it, if it wasn't already broken. He cries out in pain and tries to position his body to get off a clean punch with his good hand, but gets side-tracked because she's biting his bad hand, crushing the bones between her teeth. As he screams and tries to pull it free, she twists her body and attempts to catch him with another well-placed kick to the ribs, but misses.

He's too close, so she opens her mouth and releases his hand even as he's trying to pull it from her teeth, which causes him to stumble backwards ten or twelve inches, or, to put it another way, directly into her range. And although she only manages to land one rib kick, it's a big one. He crumples to the floor, curses, and crawls back to the foot of the bed, making sure to stay low enough to avoid her lethal legs. When he gets to his feet he's angrier than Fred Goldman, after O.J.'s acquittal.

Unfortunately for Darrell, he's lost the gun. He sees it on the bed before Callie does, but she finds it soon enough to kick it to the floor. It hits and does NOT discharge, like guns do in the movies, but when Darrell runs to grab it he accidentally pulls the trigger and sends a 147-grain hollow point into, and possibly through, the front wall of Room 216 at the Fontaine Hotel.

"Shit!" he yells. "*Shit!*" He points the gun at Joey and says, "Cuff yourself, asshole. *Now!* Or I swear to God I'll shoot you dead."

"Who are you?" Joey says. "Where's my money?"

"Cuff yourself!"

When he does, Darrell pulls him to his feet and says, "Let's go, asshole."

"Where are you taking me?" Joey says.

"To your car."

They exit the room. Callie watches the door closing behind them. At the last second, Darrell pushes it back open and says, "You didn't think I'd forget you, did you, Sweet Thing? You treated me piss-poorly, and that's a fact. I *do* think if we had a little more time together you would a' warmed up to me, but you know I can't just leave you there like that, so..."

He takes careful aim...shoots her, then leaves.

Chapter 11

CREED'S ON THE speaker instantly. "How bad is it?

Callie says nothing.

"Callie? Talk to me!"

She clears her voice. "You know why men get married?"

He breathes a sigh of relief. Then says, "So they won't have to dance anymore?"

"That's right. And women get married so they won't have to fuck anymore."

"Trudy's different."

"We're *all* different. Until we're not."

"I take it you survived the gunshot."

"The good news? My hand's still attached to my arm. The bad news? I can't feel it."

"Darrell was what, 20 feet away? Thank God he can't shoot. Wiggle your fingers."

"I thought I *was*."

"Try again."

She does.

"Much better," Creed says. "What was he using, hollow points?"

"I think so."

"Bullet could've fragmented into your eyes."

Callie looks at the bracelet. "What's this thing made of?"

"I have no idea, but I'm glad you wore it."

"I promised I would."

"And you always keep your promises."

"Donovan?"

"Yeah?"

"When you run into Darrell, don't assume he can't shoot."

"After what I just witnessed?"

"You got it wrong. He wasn't trying to kill me; he was aiming at the chain between my cuffs and the bedpost, to set me free. Joey bumped him at the last second. I'm lucky to be alive."

"He shot you by mistake?"

"That's right."

"And yet there's no wound, no blood."

Callie frowns, closes her eyes, knows where he's going, doesn't want to hear it.

Creed says, "Did I just hear you say you're lucky to be alive?"

"No."

"See, this is the beauty of living in the age of recording devices. Give me just a sec to rewind and....Ah! Here we go." He replays her voice saying, "Joey bumped him at the last

209

second. I'm lucky to be alive." He rewinds again and replays, "What's this fucking thing made of?" Then fast-forwards to: "I'm lucky to be alive." He replays it: "I'm lucky to be alive."

Callie says, "Fuck you."

Creed laughs. "Which of us should tell Trudy you got your good luck before midnight?"

"Neither."

He laughs again. "Still. The snakes? The bracelet? Are you a believer yet?"

"Not even close. You?"

"Not yet," Creed says, "and I've seen twice as much as you. But you gotta admit—"

"Don't you have work to do? And fast?"

"I do. Just wanted to make sure you were okay. Sit tight, I'll check in soon."

"Meanwhile, send Ben Terry, okay?"

"Plan's changed. I can't spare him just yet. Sit tight. Give me two minutes."

"You don't think hotel security's on the way?"

"They don't have security."

"Someone will have called the police."

"Yeah, probably. I'll get the geeks to intercept them."

"Donovan?"

"Yeah?"

"I'm sorry. I know you were counting on me to keep him busy."

"You couldn't have predicted Darrell would pop in."

"Thanks. Quick question: how many towns are within fifty miles of Roanoke?"

"I don't know."

"If you had to guess."

"Twenty?"

"Can your geeks look it up when they get a chance?"

"Of course."

Six minutes pass before Creed's back on the speaker. "This could be the craziest night of my life," he says. "It could also be my last."

"What's with the snakes?"

"According to Trudy?"

"I was hoping for a scientific opinion."

"We're fresh out of those. But Trudy believes Hawley summoned the snakes to protect our family."

"Of course she does. Do you really intend to call that poor child Hawley for the rest of her life?"

"Why not? You think they'll tease her at school?"

"*I* would have."

"Yeah, but you weren't afraid of snakes. Hang on a sec. Okay, here you go: my geeks just texted there are two hundred and nine towns within fifty miles of Roanoke. Why do you care?"

"We were talking about coincidences."

"So?"

"Try this on for size: Darrell drives to Roanoke, because that's where your attorney filed the marriage papers. His truck gets impounded, so he hitches a ride, planning to steal the guy's car, but passes out and wakes up in *Charlottesville*, the exact city where Sadie and I happen to be. With more than two hundred towns to choose from, what are the chances the car Darrell intends to steal breaks down in *Charlottesville?*"

"It's even crazier when you consider—"

"Let me finish. Darrell needs to find a car that works, so out of all the places he could steal one in Charlottesville, he chooses a *hotel*?"

"That's what he said."

"How many hotels, motels, lodges, and inns would you guess are in the general Charlottesville area?"

"From booking that very room, I know there are at least thirty."

"So, out of thirty possibilities, Darrell chooses the *Fontaine*, the same hotel you did. You know how many rooms this hotel has?"

"About a hundred."

"Out of the hundred rooms Darrell could break into hoping to steal a car, he picked Room 214, which happens to be connected to the room you booked for Sadie. And he chose to *do* so at the *exact* time we needed him *not* to."

"You done with this?"

"I'm waiting for you to calculate the odds."

"Simple. They're approximately...impossible to one. Especially when you consider Darrell's hypothesis was wrong."

"How so?"

"He assumed Charlottesville was within fifty miles of Roanoke, but he was unconscious longer than he thought, because Charlottesville's a hundred twenty miles from Roanoke, which means there are ten thousand towns that car could have broken down in, so...*shit!*"

"What's wrong?"

"What else? Another fuck up. I'll check back when I can."

PART SEVEN:
Donovan Creed

Chapter 1

WHILE WATCHING CALLIE'S drama unfold in the hotel room, I called my young bomb expert, Joe Penny, and told him to get out of Joey's van.

"I'm not finished!" he said. "Not even close."

"Doesn't matter. Joey's being kidnapped. They'll be at the van in a minute or two. You've got to abort. Grab your shit, start walking north. I'll stay on the line."

While Joe cussed and gathered his tools, I used a different disposable phone to call Ben Terry. By the time I ended that call, Joe was back on the phone, walking quickly. His equipment was heavy, his breathing labored, as he asked, "Where's Ben?"

"On the way. Keep walking north, he'll pick you up. Then—*Fuck! Damn* it!"

"What's wrong?"

"He just shot Callie!"

"*What? Who* did?

"The kidnapper."

"Is she *okay?*"

"I don't know. Stay focused. When Ben picks you up, double back to the van, let me know when Joey and Darrell get in."

"Darrell?"

"The kidnapper. Stay close to the van, follow wherever it goes. I'll get back to you when I can."

As it turned out, Callie was okay. Saved by Trudy's bracelet, if you can imagine! I talked to her long enough to make sure she was unhurt, and she talked to me long enough to let me know I was probably going to have a sexless marriage. I told her I couldn't spare anyone to set her free just yet, then I called the recently kidnapped Joseph Asad, aka "Joey", but his phone went to voicemail.

I wasn't surprised.

It would have been difficult for Darrell to stop in the middle of a shooting/kidnapping/carjacking to answer Asad's phone. So I called Joe Penny and told him Callie was alive and kicking. Literally.

"Thank God!" he said. "Does she need medical treatment?"

"No. Believe it or not, the bullet hit her bracelet. She's not even bleeding."

"Her *bracelet?* What the fuck's it made of?"

"That's the big question. Where are you?"

"Still waiting on Ben. You sure they're taking Joey's van?"

"Positive. But let's call him Asad from now on."

"Why?"

"You're Joe, he's Joey. We'll be on group calls soon, and I don't want anyone to get confused."

"You could call me Penny and call him Joey."

"Work with me. You're Joe, he's Asad. Let's talk about the bomb. What are we up against?"

"I wasn't in there long enough to give you specifics. But it's bullshit."

That surprised me. "It's not *real?*"

"Oh, it's real enough. It's just not very powerful."

"It's supposed to be a nuclear weapon."

"That part's true."

"Then what am I missing?"

"It's the Auto-Tune version."

"Dumb it down for me."

"I was. In the hierarchy of singers, you'd put a handful at the top and call them legendary. Next would be great ones, then good, then decent. Then the quality drops to average, below-average, poor, bad, terrible, and at the very bottom are those who rely on—"

"Auto-Tune."

"You got it."

"So the nuclear bomb Asad's transporting in his van turned out to be a piece of shit?"

"In the hierarchy of nuclear weapons? Yes. It's an IND, an improvised nuclear device, built from stolen components. I'm guessing the payload's a kiloton, with untested nuclear material."

"Untested?"

"It's hard for terrorists—especially in the US—to acquire enough fissile material to create a reliable nuclear explosion."

"Is it operational?"

"It appears to be."

"Assuming it detonates, how much damage are we talking about?"

"Best guess? A mile, possibly more."

"That's *it*? A *mile*? Including fallout?"

"The destructive force of a kiloton bomb includes air blast, heat, initial radiation, secondary radiation, and ground shock. The air blast kills half the people within a 900-foot circumference of the blast site. The heat produces a million-degree fireball that fatally burns half the people within 2,700 feet. Initial radiation kills half the people in a half-mile radius in the first minute. Secondary radiation is the first hour after the explosion. It's weather-determined, but three to four miles downwind seems worst-case. But even that should dissipate quickly."

"What about ground shock?"

"Six-and-a-half to seven on the Richter Scale, at the epicenter."

"But it's not much of a bomb?"

"For a nuclear weapon? No. But for a terrorist act it's massive. Terrifying. Unprecedented."

"Compare it to the Oklahoma City bomb."

"That one was non-nuclear, with a yield of zero-point-zero-zero-two. It killed 168 people, injured 700, destroyed 324 buildings in a 16-block radius, and caused $650 million worth of damage."

"And the bomb in Asad's van?"

"Roughly five hundred times more powerful."

"You're sure?"

"At a minimum. You said he's planning to blow up the White House?"

"Is it possible?"

"You're joking, right?"

"Humor me."

"The west wing of the White House is only 370 feet from 17th Street."

"Yeah, but it's flanked by the Eisenhower Office Building. Wouldn't that take the brunt of the explosion?"

"It would, but we're still talking total devastation."

"What about my original scenario? The one in my report?"

"The attack from H Street? Slam dunk. It's directly behind the White House, offers a straight shot through Lafayette Square."

"And it's eight hundred feet?"

"Yeah. Eight hundred-twenty, to be exact. I think I see Ben pulling up."

"Good. How far are you guys from the van?"

"Block-and-a-half."

"Let me know when you see them."

"Will do."

As he climbed into Ben's car I said, "Just to be clear, you're saying Asad's bomb could level the White House?"

"And then some. Assuming it detonates. But remember, it's an IND, and just as likely to fizzle. But even a fizzle would disperse enough radioactive material to be classified as a dirty bomb. So, what's the plan?"

"I'll establish contact with Darrell and talk him into stopping somewhere long enough for you to do your magic."

He laughed. "You're going to talk a kidnapper into walking away from his escape vehicle?"

"That's right."

"With his victim?"

"Yup."

"For a solid hour?"

"That's the plan."

"How you gonna manage that?"

"I'll think of something."

"Can I ask a stupid question?" Joe said. "Why not just kill Asad and tow the van to a safe location where I can dismantle the bomb and save fifty to a hundred thousand American lives?"

I sighed. "I *want* the bomb to detonate."

Chapter 2

"YOU WANT THE bomb to detonate?" Joe Penny repeated, incredulously.

"Yes. But somewhere safe."

Joe pauses a long time before asking, "Have we defected?"

Joe's as loyal as they come, but that doesn't mean he needs to know everything that goes on in my crazy world. Instead of answering, I said, "Stay close to the van. I'll check back soon." Then I dictated a text message to Asad's phone, knowing Darrell would see it:

> Darrell, I understand you're looking for me.
> Let's talk. –Donovan Creed.

Within seconds, my phone rang.

"Is this the asshole who stole my wife?"

"Nope. This is Donovan Creed."

"Same difference. This is Darrell."

"So I figured."

"You know how I come to be in Virginia?"

"I think so. Trudy warned me."

"What'd she say, exactly?"

"She said, 'Every time Satan's toilet overflows, Darrell pops up.'"

"You think that's funny?"

"Yeah, but I'm biased."

"You'll *be* bi-assed by the time *I* get through with you. What made you think you could marry my wife and get away with it?"

"The marriage license. The ceremony. The preacher. The witnesses. Before that? The divorce papers. The fact she's your ex-wife."

"That ain't how *I* see it."

"Then maybe you should get your eyes checked."

"Maybe I will. Until then, chew on this, Creed: there ain't *nothin'* you can do to Trudy that I ain't done to her first."

"Yeah there is: I can make her happy."

"You ain't got a *clue*, do you! I bet she ain't told you *half* the shit I done to her or what she done to me. There ain't one square inch a' her body I ain't seen, touched, licked, sniffed, or fucked. How you like *that*, city boy?"

I say nothing.

He says, "How you feel about all them blow jobs she give me?"

"I guess she had to practice somewhere."

"You know what I just realized? Trudy ain't told you *shit* about her and me!"

"She told me enough."

"Like what?"

"Like how you smelled so bad she had to feed you with a slingshot."

"Fuck *you*, Asshole! You best believe I'm comin' for you! And when I get there..."

"Yeah?"

"I'm gonna be all over you like a bad rash on a big ass."

"See you then."

"Damn straight you will! ...Uh...where the fuck *are* you?"

"Stay where you are. I'll call you back."

"I can't. I'm in the middle of a...situation. So here's what's gonna happen: I'm gonna start drivin', and you're gonna tell me where to go."

"I'll call you."

"Wait! You know where I am?"

"Yeah. Start driving."

"Which direction?"

"Doesn't matter. I'll tell you how to find me when I call back."

"You better, or I'll be hotter than hell's furnace on Judgment Day. You understand?"

"Not really."

I hung up and called Sadie Sharp.

Chapter 3

"WHERE'S CALLIE?" SADIE asked.

"She's been shot."

"*What?*"

"You *care?* Or are you just surprised?"

"Mildly surprised. Is she dead?"

"Not yet, but I can put her on my list if you like. You're still at the top though, for shafting me."

"Callie said you wouldn't mind if she took my place because I would have screwed things up and ruined your plan."

"She's right. But *you* should've been shot, not her."

"I suppose you'll have plenty of opportunities to shoot me."

"I only need one...Or I can wipe your slate clean."

"You won't do that."

"Where are you now?"

"You don't *know?*"

"I do, but I'm hoping you'll tell me the truth."

"Callie said you hid a transmitter in my car, but you know what I think?"

"You think she's wrong. You think I'm lying."

"I do. Or you wouldn't have asked where I was."

"You require proof."

"That's right."

I took a deep breath. "Okay, but I'm only going to do this once."

"Go ahead then."

"You're in your car, heading south on 27."

She paused a moment. "You're just guessing."

"You're passing 16th street as we speak. What's surprising, you're not wearing the wig and sunglasses I told you to wear. Even more surprising, you're sitting in the passenger seat, and some guy named Mike is driving. Your phone's on speaker, and he's staring at you like he's having second thoughts about going to the hotel to protect Callie. By the way, that's your cue to talk to me, Mike."

"What's up?" he said.

"You're in this now, Mike. You and Sadie are a team."

"I don't think so."

"Think again."

"You can't track us both. I can pull over, let myself off, vanish into the night."

"You think I didn't get your license plate when she pulled in behind your car? You think I haven't run your data? You're Michael R. Singletary, 35 years old, you live in an apartment at 1215 Eastern Parkway, and you work at Carson Electric on Millstone Drive. You're divorced. Your ex-wife, Veronica, now goes by Ronnie, according to her

Facebook page. You've been arrested for domestic violence, and for violating a restraining order. You have no kids, but your sister, Donna, has three: Jimmy, Dale, and Carrie Ann. I can kill all these people before midnight, Mike, and if you'd like me to prove it, I can start by putting a bullet in your left arm right now."

"H-how could you possibly—"

"Or if you'd prefer—and this is something I highly recommend—I could simply fire a warning shot in the back seat of Sadie's car."

"Go ahead, if you can," Sadie said.

I pressed a button and a bullet fired crosswise, from the backseat passenger's armrest to the opposite door. Mike and Sadie screamed. Mike swerved the car, jumped the curb, and would have killed them both, had I not taken control of the brakes and brought their car to a safe stop.

"H-how d-did you d-do that?" Mike said.

"Does it really matter?"

"N-n-n—"

Sadie frowned, finished his thought. "Not really."

"That's right," I said. "The only thing that matters is, are you going to cooperate or am I going to kill you."

Sadie said, "What do we have to do?"

"Get in the blue van."

"What blue van?"

Chapter 4

NOW ON THE phone with Darrell, I direct him to Sadie and Mike's location.

"This ain't no joyride, Creed," he says. "I'm lookin' to come get Trudy. I'm gonna march in your front door and take back what's mine."

"Are you aware there are currently a million snakes surrounding my property?"

"I ain't afraid of snakes. I *eat* 'em."

"Of course you do. But if you want to meet me tonight, you'll have to do it my way."

"Who are these people?"

"You only need to know where they are. Take Highway 27 to Sixteenth Street."

"I ain't from here. I don't know where them streets are."

"Tell me where you are and I'll direct you."

He does, and I do. When Mike and Sadie get in the van I tell Darrell to pass the phone to Sadie.

"Why?"

"I'll talk to her, and she'll relay the information to you."

"How about you just talk to me?"

"I'll talk to you when I see you."

He gives Sadie the phone. She says, "I'm here."

I say, "I don't have any surveillance equipment in the van, so you'll have to be my eyes and ears."

"Okay."

"Tell Darrell to go straight for two blocks, then turn left on Carpenter and drive slowly."

When she gives him those instructions I say, "We're stalling for time, Sadie, so I need you to tell me anything you see out the front windshield that's unique."

"What do you mean?"

"Anything out of the ordinary."

"You mean like a lady walking a bunch of dogs in the middle of the night?"

"What made you ask that?"

"I'm looking at her."

"Perfect. Tell Darrell when he turns left on Carpenter to drive a block and park first chance he gets. Then wait for my instructions."

I hang up, call Joe Penny: "You following the van?"

"Yeah. We're two blocks back."

"You see a lady walking some dogs?"

He pauses. "Yeah."

"Okay. Stay back. When the van turns left on Carpenter, move up and talk to the dog lady."

"About what?"

I tell him, then I call Sadie and tell her what to do. Predictably, Darrell raises hell, but he's got no choice. When they all leave the van I call Callie.

"I thought you forgot me," she says.

"Sorry."

"How's your plan coming along?"

"Like a fire drill at clown college."

"Does that mean I'll have to stay like this a while?"

"Yeah. Sorry."

"Can we talk about Sadie?"

"What do you want to know?"

"Did you know Joey was planning to kill her?"

"No."

"Would you have let him?"

"Yes."

"Why?"

"I needed the time."

"This must be one hell of a mission."

"It is."

"Tell me."

"I'm allowing a terrorist to detonate a nuclear bomb."

"Where?"

"Rural Virginia. Someplace safe."

"When?"

"Tonight."

"Why?"

"To protect the country."

"Because it'll force the administration to implement your safety measures?"

"They only respond to public outcry."

"You're not the mastermind."

"No. But after uncovering the plot, I felt I might be able to contain it. Shock the country into being more vigilant."

"How many people are you willing to sacrifice?"

"None. But some are going to die."

"Joey?"

"For sure."

"What about Sadie?"

"She's a loose end."

"You were always going to kill her."

"Yes."

"I assumed you killed her husband?"

"Not me personally, but yeah, he's dead."

"You could have told her. I don't think she would've batted an eye."

"I agree."

"She's got some sort of mental condition."

"She does. But she also has an amazing capacity for self-preservation."

"Is that why you chose her? You wanted someone you could control?"

"I chose her because she was married to Rick. When I learned about her condition I realized I couldn't control her, so I had to settle for directing her."

"How did Rick figure into it?"

"He hired me to kill his neighbor."

"Carol?"

"No. Carol's husband, Kenny."

"Why?"

"Rick and Carol were having an affair, but Carol took it more seriously. She saw them running off into the sunset together."

"So you killed Kenny, but why Carol?"

"She was unhappy Rick planned to stay with Sadie after all, and threatened to tell the cops about the affair."

"Her word against his."

"Except that she told Sadie about the affair. Rick didn't know at the time, but when he found out he knew if the cops questioned Sadie, she'd give them enough information to make him a suspect. He was afraid of losing his job."

Callie says, "You're keeping me here on purpose."

"It's not personal."

"You're afraid if you let me go I'll try to save Sadie."

"I know you will. She hired you to protect her. When you take a job you do the job. No exceptions."

"You and I have a lot of history."

"We do."

"We've saved each other's lives numerous times."

"We have."

"Does that earn me a favor?"

"I can't spare her life, Callie. Her testimony puts me on death row."

"I understand that. I agree she has to die."

"Then what's the favor?"

"Let me be the one to kill her."

That throws me. All I can think to say is, "Why?"

"Think about it."

It only takes me a second. "If I kill her it means you failed to protect her."

"Exactly."

I think it over a minute, then say, "Okay. I'll do my best."

"Thanks."

"It has to be tonight, Callie."

"I'll kill her an hour after she gets here. You have my word."

PART EIGHT:
Joseph "Joey" Asad

Chapter 1

Four Hours Earlier...

JOEY HAD IT all planned out: tonight—his last night on earth—would be spent in the arms of his beautiful wife, Isha. He'd reserved a fancy restaurant, booked a limo. After dinner, there'd be laughter, dancing, champagne. The night would end with sex.

Lots of sex.

To make up for all the sex he'd been missing lately.

With Isha.

Only it didn't work out that way.

At five p.m., Joey got a call from his cousin, Amer, who said, "The president inexplicably returned a day early from Camp David. Our window of opportunity has narrowed. I need you to move the van west of D.C. immediately."

Joey wanted to know why.

Amer said, "The president plans to leave the White House at noon tomorrow, a full day ahead of schedule. Which means we need to attack at eight a.m."

"I have plans tonight."

"When men make plans, Allah laughs."

Amer told Joey to order a cab immediately, meet him at the Flaherty Hotel in Georgetown. From there, Amer would drive Joey to the van, Joey would follow him back to the hotel. The cousins would stay in separate rooms at the hotel tonight and bomb the White House in the morning after performing ablutions.

Joey broke the news to Isha about the canceled plans.

She was, to put it mildly, upset.

He apologized, attempted to have sex with her, but she refused. He didn't blame her for being angry, and of course, she had no idea he was giving his life tomorrow for the cause. He wished he could tell her, but if she happened to be singled out for interrogation and had any foreknowledge of the event the authorities would be able to tell.

Still, he deserved sex from his own wife, did he not?

It crossed his mind to force her, but he discarded the thought, knowing if he did the angels would hesitate to pray for him, or speak to God on his behalf. So he left, angry and frustrated, without saying a word as to where he was going or when he'd be back.

He could wait.

Isha was gorgeous, but she had a bad attitude. Refusing to have sex with her *husband*? Oh, how he ached to beat that godless Western influence out of her! But it wasn't an option, as Joey couldn't take a chance on drawing attention to himself. And anyway he knew eventually Isha would be among the members of his household in heaven, at which point she would desire him day and night.

Once in heaven, he'll punish her by making her wait her turn, as there will be either 70 or 72 virgins ahead of her. Joey's unclear if the number is 70 or 72, since it varies depending on who's delivering the message on any given day. Still, he'd be content with 70, knowing two wives are also included in the celestial package.

Tomorrow, upon entering the kingdom, he'll make a point to ask that Isha be placed in his household in paradise, and knows that wish will be granted.

Joseph "Joey" Asad, age 24, is a Syrian national, passing as an American, with an American passport. Eighteen months ago, after receiving substantial training, he was given an American-born Syrian wife named Isha, an apartment, and enough cash to survive until called to martyrdom. Now that his training has been completed and his mission announced, he's been paid $50,000, most of which is currently in Isha's account, save for the $5,000 he kept for himself in case of emergency.

Joey smiled. Perhaps he could use that money to amuse himself tonight.

Western suicide bombers have far more latitude than their Eastern counterparts. Overseas, the suicide bomber is isolated from family, friends, and even his terror cell for a full three weeks prior to the attack. He (or she) is told nothing about the mission until moments before carrying it out. His final days are spent watching propaganda films that detail the vast rewards given to martyrs in paradise. When he finally receives his mission, he prays, records a video testament, and drinks water which—without his knowledge—is probably laced with drugs.

But here in the West, who's going to tell him and Amer they can't enjoy themselves the night before nuking the White House?

Chapter 2

HOURS LATER, WITH the van safely parked behind the Flaherty Hotel, Amer said, "One of us must guard the van tonight, but that doesn't mean we can't have fun. Mine will be delayed, since I need to visit with the local Imams, but you can start immediately. Here."

"What is this you have given me?"

"The phone number of a local service. Call them, tell them what type of woman you want, and they'll send her over."

"Is it safe, cousin?"

"In what way?"

"Revealing our location."

Amer laughs. "You worry too much. You're a businessman, spending the night. You could be any man, anywhere."

"Can this agency be trusted?"

"I wouldn't put you in danger, cousin. I've used them myself."

"You *have?*"

"Several times. Their women are beautiful, and up for anything."

"*Anything?*"

Amer looks at him. "What is it you'd want her to do?"

Joey blushes. "I would be embarrassed to ask."

"I'll call them for you."

"Really?"

"Of course. What are you seeking? Tonight, the world is yours."

"I am not overly particular."

"Well, I'm sure they'll make every attempt to accommodate your wishes. You should ask for something."

"I would not know what to say."

"You still like blondes?"

"Yes, of course."

"All right then! I'll ask for a blonde."

"Wonderful! Thank you."

"You are most welcome, cousin." He turns to leave.

Joey says, "Ideally?"

Amer turns around. "Yes?"

"She would be pretty."

"Of course. A pretty blonde. Why not?"

"Uh...perhaps we should ask for beautiful."

"A beautiful blonde. Very well."

"And young."

"Young?"

"With blue eyes."

"Is the eye color so important?"

"I am just stating what would be ideal."

"Well, we can ask." He turns to leave.

"Uh...."

"Yes?"

"Anal."

"Excuse me?"

"She should be into anal sex."

"You're narrowing the field."

"If the world is truly mine, she would be a young, beautiful blue-eyed blonde, who loves anal."

Amer frowns. "Anything else?"

"I would also like very much to handcuff her to the bedpost."

"That might be a tall order."

"I would also like to beat her, and rape her violently."

Amer stares at his cousin a long time. "Perhaps we should leave that last part out of the description. Once she's handcuffed, you can do whatever you wish, within reason. In other words, you don't want a woman screaming in your hotel room. If she screams and someone comes to her aid, it could jeopardize the mission."

"Perhaps we should simply say rough sex?"

"If she's willing. But again, if she cries out—"

"I understand."

"Do you even *have* handcuffs?"

"Three sets. In my bag."

"How did you—"

"I ordered them online. I had hoped to handcuff Isha tonight."

"With *three* sets of handcuffs?" Amer gives him a funny look. Then says, "Here's your room key. Get comfortable while I call the service. I'll let you know what they say."

"Thank you."

Ten minutes later, Amer comes to Joey's room, hands him a cell phone. "From now on, use this phone. It's disposable. Untraceable."

"How many minutes does it have?"

"More than you do, my friend."

They laugh.

Joey asks, "What did the agency say to you?"

"They have a girl. Sadie."

"Blonde?"

"Highlights. Brown eyes, not blue."

"Young?"

"Reasonably young. Early twenties."

"Anal?"

"Yes. And she's open to handcuffs."

Joey smiles. "At what time should I expect her arrival?"

"They'll call you soon to let you know."

"On this phone?"

"Yes. Enjoy your time."

"What about you?"

"I'll be back by eleven. And yes, I requested a girl for myself from the same agency."

"What type?"

"I'm not so particular. I only requested a hooker."

"Maybe they will send you a man."

Amer smiles. "Let's hope not."

They hug.

Amer says, "We'll meet at sunrise, to perform ablutions."

Joey nods. "Here? My room?"

"Yes. See you then."

Twenty minutes after Amer leaves, Joey's phone rings. It's the man from the agency, telling Joey that while Sadie's happy to meet him, he'll have to come to her. She's in Room 216 at the Fontaine Hotel, in Charlottesville, Virginia, and can see him at ten p.m.

"That is an hour's drive!" Joey says. "Unacceptable. I need her to come to my hotel room, here in Georgetown."

"If you'd given me a week I could've gotten you anything you want," the man says. "Any time, any place. You want a one-armed, tap-dancing, two-headed lesbian with hairy tits? No problem. How about a death row prison groupie who'll fuck you on a skateboard while singing *Che Gelida Manina* from *La Bohème*? For us, it's anything you say, sir! Or perhaps you'd prefer a thumbless zoo keeper who's so skinny you can look in her asshole and see the back of her bellybutton. Ordinarily, my response would be 'Yes, absolutely.' But this is short notice, and Congress is in session."

"What does *that* mean?"

"It means apart from Sadie, we're fresh out of gorgeous young blondes who are into beat-downs, handcuffs and anal sex. That said, I *do* have two hair-lipped trannies, a cross-eyed midget with hair plugs, and a broken-down granny whose tits have fallen so low she has to get her mammograms from a podiatrist. On the bright side, they can be at your hotel room within the hour."

"*They?*"

"These four only work as a group."

Joey holds the phone away from his ear, stares at it a moment, then returns it and says, "Do you have a picture of Sadie?"

"Yes, of course. Shall I send it straight away?"

"Yes please."

He does, and Joey's pleasantly surprised. "Very well, tell her I will double her fee if she comes to Georgetown tonight."

"It won't do any good."

"I see where this is going. Please inform the whelp that I will *triple* her fee."

"You don't understand. For Sadie, it's not about the money. The woman loves to fuck!"

"It appears she has made an appropriate career choice. Many young people do not, in my opinion. This is a good thing."

"It's not good, it's *great!* Sadie'll fuck anything that moves or stands still. Anything with a pulse. A moose, a maggot, or anything in-between. A French fry. A belt buckle. I swear she'd fuck a *fart* if it originated in Charlottesville. But she won't travel."

"Why is that, do you think?"

"She's a germaphobe."

"A what?"

"She has a pathological fear of germs and contamination. She believes all vehicles are dirty. The seats, the door handles, the head rests. She can't abide them, and won't touch them."

"To recap: this women will gladly fuck a moose, man, or maggot but resists all forms of transportation due to germs?"

"That's correct."

"I can sympathize."

"You can? Well, that's great, because she'll make you happy, my friend. I guarantee it. In fact—"

"Yes?"

"I probably shouldn't say this, but she's into pain."

Joey perks up. "How do you mean?"

"She likes rough sex."

"*How* rough?"

"I don't quite know how to answer that, but she's obviously durable."

"Can you offer an example?"

"She was once fucked completely out of context by a *New York Times* reporter."

"Who hasn't been?" Joey says. "And yet, she sounds spectacular. Do you have any nude photos of her?"

"*Excuse* me?"

"Any photos of Sadie without clothing?"

"*Are you kidding me?* Of *course* not! What type of person do you *take* me for?"

"Uh...a pimp?"

"Fair enough."

"Whoremonger?"

"Certainly."

"Hustler?"

"Yes."

"Panderer? Flesh-peddler?"

"Absolutely. But I'm no *voyeur!*"

"Sorry. I did not mean to offend you."

"Very well, my good man. I accept your apology with peace and love. Where were we?"

"Sadie."

"Yes, of course. So anyway, it seems to me you've got two choices: you can drive to Charlottesville and have the time of your life or you can spend a quiet evening with Mother Thumb and her four lovely daughters."

"Can you repeat the details of the proposed engagement?"

"Ten o'clock, Room 216, Fontaine Hotel, Charlottesville, Virginia. What do you say?"

Joey thinks a moment. While he'd love to spend his last night on Earth beating the shit out of Sadie, he can't take a cab to Charlottesville and leave the van unguarded. On the other hand, if he *takes* the van he'd be guarding it all the way there and back. And if he's *with* the van, what could possibly go wrong?

"I shall accept the arrangement!"

"Excellent! You've made a wise choice."

Chapter 3

AT TEN P.M. Joey taps on the door of Room 216 and is stunned by the beauty of the goddess who opens the door. He checks the photo the man at the agency sent. Not that he's complaining, but he needs to make certain this is the same girl.

But it can't be!

After a moment of prompting, she admits her name is Callie, not Sadie, and she's a substitute. But is he complaining?

Absolutely not!

She's indescribably beautiful. More than he could have hoped for, although if he's being picky, her eyes—while dazzling—are gray.

Callie's phone rings. Normally he'd insist she give him her complete attention, and in fact he does tell her he's on a strict timetable, but she brushes him off with a wink and a smile, and he's so smitten with her beauty he's content to drink vodka from a miniature bottle and watch her mouth move as she speaks. When she's finished, she apologizes and says "...from here on out...I'm all yours!"

Joey smiles. "You like it rough?"

"Within reason," she says.

They agree to a safe word, *persimmon*, which is bullshit, since he intends to beat the piss out of her, then rape and kill her.

After handcuffing her to the headboard, he steps back to admire his work, then tells her it's going to be a special night. He explains why, and ends his speech by telling her she's going to pay for his sins with her blood.

She handles the news surprisingly well: there's no crying, whimpering, or begging. No screaming.

If anything, she seems curious. She asks if he's planning to cut her up, as if that would be okay. He takes a moment to wonder what sort of twisted fuck he's dealing with, then says, "I'm planning to kill you."

Again, no apparent concern from this gorgeous hooker, which makes him wonder what sort of men she's been with in the past. Her only question is why. But when he tells her, she says, "I don't think so, asshole," and before he can respond, everything goes dark. When he regains consciousness, it's as if he woke up in the middle of a scene from the movie *Deliverance*. He sees a primitive man—a hillbilly—in the room. The man has an odd, backwoods accent, and he's trying to rape the hooker, Callie.

Joey coughs a couple times, tries to clear his head. Spots his bag on the chair and thinks: *if I can just get the gun...but* it's too late. The hillbilly also sees the bag, grabs it first, finds the gun and the third set of handcuffs.

Joey's head is foggy. He slips in and out of consciousness several times until the hillbilly points the gun at him and says, "Cuff yourself, Asshole."

The hillbilly—Darrell, if Joey heard correctly—pulls Joey to his feet and says, "Let's go, Asshole."

"Where are you taking me?"

"To your car."

Shit! He's being kidnapped. Joey can't fathom how his luck turned so bad so quick. Was it too much to ask for on his last night on earth? A little pussy and some liquor? He remembers what his cousin, Amer, said: "When men make plans, Allah laughs."

As they leave the room, to Joey's surprise, Darrell shoots Callie. As they move down the hall, Darrell says, "What's your name?"

"Joey."

"You don't look like no Joey. What're you, French?"

Joey gives him a look. "I am an American."

"Bullshit. I halfway think you look like one a' them terrorist dudes that nuked the World Trade Center."

"A nuclear weapon has *never* been detonated on American soil!"

"Sure they have."

"There have been none," Joey says, adamantly. "Of this I am certain."

"You're full of shit, Frenchie. You never heard of the Nevada Test Site?"

"No."

"Pacific Provin' Grounds? Our government's conducted a thousand nuclear tests at them places alone. Not to mention Alaska, Colorado, and other places I can't even remember."

"I am neither French, nor terrorist. I am a U.S. citizen."

"Prove it!"

"I have a driver's license."

"*Driver's* license?" Darrell laughs. "*Anyone* can buy a fuckin' driver's license. Turn left, we're takin' the steps. Who plays quarterback for the Cowboys?"

"I do not follow sports."

"*Aha!* I *knew* it!"

"Ask me something else."

"Turn left. Now go straight. Open the door, to the parking lot. What's your favorite TV show?"

"Jeopardy."

"*What?*"

"Meet the Press? Face the Nation?"

"Shut the fuck up! I have half a mind to kick your ass right now."

"What is wrong?"

"You're a Communist!"

"I am *not*."

"Tell that to the judge, Frenchie."

"Which judge?"

"Where's your car?"

"I do not have a—"

Darrell presses the key. The van's headlights flicker. "*Sweet!*" he says. He slides the cargo door open and shoves Joey inside. Sees the tarp, says, "What the fuck's *that?*"

252

Joey decides not to tell him it's a nuclear weapon. "Scrap," he says.

Darrell uses Joey's phone to illuminate the cargo. "I never seen scrap that glowed in the dark. You know what I think this is?"

"What?"

"Some sort of fancy-ass still. You cookin' moonshine, Frenchie?"

"I have repeatedly told you I am not French."

Darrell says, "I can find someone back home to gimme cash for this."

"It is worthless."

"I don't think so, Frenchie. If it *was*, I reckon you wouldn't be haulin' it around, all covered up. The tarp *alone's* gotta be worth five, ten bucks."

"Let me go. You can keep the money. Five thousand U.S. dollars. I will not report it."

"I already *got* your money, asshole. *And* your van. *And* your gun."

"Please let me go. I need to be somewhere later tonight. It is urgent."

"You know what my mama used to say?"

"I need to—"

"Mama used to say 'Tell me what you need and I'll tell you how to live without it.' Do beavers eat fish?"

"What?"

"It's a simple question, Frenchie. Do beavers eat fish?"

"Beavers...are primarily nocturnal, semi-aquatic rodents. They have broad, flat tails and sharp teeth used for cutting down trees with which they build dams. They live in rivers, lakes, ponds, and streams, so they most certainly eat fish."

"*Wrong!* You ain't no American. Probably never drank a domestic beer in your life."

The phone suddenly beeps with a text, which Darrell reads out loud:

> *Darrell, I understand you're looking for me.*
> *Let's talk. –Donovan Creed.*

Darrell dials the number and asks, "Is this the asshole who stole my wife?"

He seems quite angry with the man named Donovan Creed. They argue a few minutes, and Darrell finally tells Joey to lie down in the back of the van and keep quiet. Then he climbs into the driver's seat and starts the engine. He hangs up and drives for several minutes until his phone rings again. It's Mr. Creed again, telling Darrell to pull over and wait for two passengers to arrive.

Two passengers?

Before long a man and woman get in the car, and astonishingly, Joey recognizes her as the woman in the photo on his phone!

Sadie!

After a brief exchange, it is determined that the man, Mike, will lie down on the floor with Joey and Sadie will ride in the front passenger seat and converse with Creed on the phone as Creed instructs them where to drive. Joey hears Sadie describing a lady walking a bunch of dogs on the sidewalk. Within minutes she tells Darrell where to park the van. When they come to a stop, Darrell forces everyone to exit the van. Then the strangest thing happens.

Chapter 4

SADIE SAYS, "WE need to walk back to Highway 27 and find the dog lady."

"Why?" Darrell asks.

"We're going to help her walk her dogs."

"*What?*"

"That's what the killer said."

"What killer?"

"The guy on the phone."

"He ain't no killer, he's my wife's husband."

She pauses. "I don't know what you want me to say, but I have it on good authority he's a hit man."

"Donovan *Creed?*"

"I don't know if that's his name, but I definitely know the killer's voice."

"It's the same guy was on the phone when I handed it to you?"

"Yes."

"Well, he ain't no killer. But I might kill *him*."

"Your wife's a bigamist?"

"Hell no! Trudy's Christian. Give me the phone."

He redials Creed's number, but gets no answer.

Sadie says, "Creed—if that's his name—was adamant."

"What's that mean?" Darrell says.

"It means he told me we had to go with the lady to walk the dogs or you wouldn't get what you want."

"This is bullshit."

"Can we just go meet the lady? Maybe she has some information."

Darrell says, "That there's a good point." He bangs the side of the van loudly and tells Joey and Mike to get out. Of course, Joey wasn't expecting the sudden sound, and for a split second he thought the bomb had detonated. It takes him a full thirty seconds to get his heart to stop racing.

As they scramble out of the van, Mike says, "What the *fuck?*"

Darrell says, "God damn it, Frenchie! Did you shit your *pants?*"

He did.

Sadie winces at the smell.

"So sorry," Joey says. "Can we take a moment to allow this woman to remove my pants and undergarments and wash them out?"

"Fuck no! You're just gonna have to walk sloppy and deal with it."

The four—Darrell, Sadie, Mike, and Joey—walk to Highway 27, turn right, and approach the lady who's attempting to walk nine dogs at the same time. When the dogs

257

get a whiff of Joey, they come at him like they've struck the mother lode. As the dogs attack, Sadie screams and the dog lady gives Joey a look of utter disdain. He fails to notice, having fallen to the ground from the force of the assault. Now the dogs are on him like sharks on chum, ripping the entire ass off his jeans. Joey shrieks in pain as the dogs sink their teeth into his flesh repeatedly, attempting to remove every last bit of soiled fabric. The harder they pull, the harder Darrell laughs. "Look at 'em goin' to town!" he hollers. "It's like he's wearin' Milk Bone underwear!"

Finally the dogs back away, content to chew their bounty and offer Joey the occasional growl. As Darrell continues to laugh, Joey moans in pain. Having grown up in Syria, where wild dogs are known to be ferocious, Joey always assumed Western dogs were as docile and weak as their owners. But never in his life has he witnessed anything as horrific and terrifying as what just occurred to him. And the hillbilly thinks it's *funny*?

He does. He says, "God help me, but I ain't laughed this hard since the pigs ate my brother!"

"This man needs medical attention," Sadie says.

Mike leans over him. "You okay, brother?"

When Joey fails to answer, Mike says, "I think he's in shock."

The dog lady says, "Why's he handcuffed?"

"He's French," Darrell says, as if that's explanation enough. Then he asks, "Have you got some information for us about Donovan Creed?"

"I do," she says.

"Let's have it."

She eyes Joey closely before saying, "I'm supposed to give each of you two dogs to walk."

"How far we goin'?"

"Montgomery Road."

"How far's that?"

"I'm not sure. It's pretty far, though."

"How long will it take to get there?"

"At least a half hour. Maybe more."

"Is that where Creed is?"

"That's my understanding."

"Someone pay you to go that far?"

"Yes."

"You know what he's tryin' to do? Tire me out so he can whip my ass when we finally get to Montgomery Road. What he don't know, I've coon hunted all night long for half my life. I got more stamina than a Viagra rabbit."

"This man's in no condition to walk," Sadie says.

"He don't have to, 'cause I got a better idea," Darrell says. "How about we load everyone in the van: us five and all the dogs."

"No!" Joey shouts, suddenly lucid. "That is too many! The van will explode!"

Darrell says, "If you was American you'd know vans don't explode when overloaded. The wheels might pop, but that's about it."

"You do not understand!" Joey says.

"I understand your bloody ass is hangin' out your pants."

Sadie removes her own phone from her jeans' pocket and calls Creed. He answers with "What's wrong?"

"I've got you on speaker. The man in handcuffs?"

"Joey? What about him?"

"He shit his pants and the dogs attacked him. He's badly hurt. Can we take him to a hospital?"

"No!" Joey shouts.

"No," Creed says. "Sit tight. I'll be back in touch."

"When?"

"An hour or so."

"That's unacceptable."

"Sorry, those are my terms."

"Fine. But you should know Darrell's already walking toward the van. He's planning to drive it here and take us all to Montgomery Road."

"Shit!" Creed says. "Okay, tell the dog lady to go about her business. Tell her thanks, but we don't need her. When Darrell comes back, climb in the van and wait for my call."

Chapter 5

"WHERE ARE YOU now?" Creed asks.

"You're on speaker again," Sadie says. "Sorry, Darrell insists."

"No problem. Where *are* you?"

"Heading toward Montgomery Road. Darrell wants to know if you're already there."

"I'm comin' for you Creed!" he hollers.

"What should I tell him?" Sadie asks.

"Ignore him and tell me when you see something out of the ordinary."

"I can hear every word you say," Darrell says.

A minute passes before Sadie says, "Four men in Groucho masks are trying to flag us down."

"Perfect."

"Excuse me?"

"Darrell, pull over," Creed says. "Find out what they want."

"What sort of cockamamie bullshit is this, Creed?" Darrell says, but he pulls over, and Sadie rolls down her window, and the men tell Sadie they're medical students, members of a band called The Swingin' Groucho's, on their way home from a gig. Their van broke down and they need a ride to the nearest gas station.

"Why are they still wearing their masks?" Creed asks.

One of the Grouchos hears Creed and says, "We don't want to be recognized."

"Why not?"

"Not only are we on full scholarships, but we've accepted grant money from the government."

"For what?"

"You'll laugh."

"I'll probably cry. But tell me anyway."

"The government's paying us to study why children fall off tricycles."

Darrell says, "How much they give you for that?"

"Three hundred twenty-eight thousand."

"*Dollars?*" Darrell says.

The Groucho nods.

Joey, thinking, *The men and women who govern this country are hopelessly insane!*

Darrell says, "For three hundred twenty-eight thousand dollars I'll push kids off tricycles all day long."

The Groucho says, "If the school finds out we're making money on the side we'll lose our funding."

"Is there a reward for squealin' you out?" Darrell says. "'cause if so, I aim to claim it."

"No reward," the Groucho says. "But can we catch a ride?"

"You're medical students?" Sadie says.

"Yes."

"Can you patch up our friend?"

"We ain't got time for this," Darrell says.

"Let them take a look at him, Darrell," Creed says. "You'll meet me soon enough."

Sadie says, "He's in the back."

"What's wrong with him?" a Groucho asks.

"He got dog-bit," Darrell says.

"I can take a quick look."

The Grouchos open the cargo door. One of them asks Darrell to flip the lights on.

"I didn't know I could," he says.

He fumbles around till he finds the right switch. "How's that?"

"Christ!" the Groucho says. "That's the worst looking ass I've ever seen!"

"You know what that tells me?" Darrell says.

"What's that?"

"You ain't met Cletus Renfro's sister, from Clayton, Kentucky."

One of the other Grouchos says, "Excuse me, but is that a *bomb?*"

Chapter 6

DARRELL SAYS, "JOEY'S a terrorist! I fuckin' *knew* it!"

Sadie screams.

Mike bolts from the van and keeps running.

The Grouchos scatter in all directions.

Creed shouts, "Darrell and Sadie, out of the van. *Now!* Asad, stay put!"

"Asad?" Darrell says.

Thirty seconds later, two men approach the van. Darrell says, "Which of you is Creed?"

"Neither, you idiot," Creed says. "I'm still on the phone, talking to you."

"Well, tell 'em to come no closer," Darrell says. "I've got a gun."

"Here's what you're going to do," Creed says. "Stand down. One of the men is going to get in the van and drive away."

Sadie says, "What about Joey?"

"We'll take care of him."

"You ain't takin' my ride," Darrell says.

"The other man will give you a ride to the meeting place."

"Why should I trust him?"

"You've got a gun. If he doesn't take you to me immediately you have my permission to shoot him."

"Don't think I won't."

PART NINE:
Callie Carpenter

Chapter 1

Eighty Minutes Later...

WHEN CREED'S VOICE finally comes on the speaker Callie says, "I take it the mission went well?"

"It did. I mean, we'll have to monitor the situation, keep an eye on radiation levels and so forth, but I'm cautiously optimistic. For the moment, at least."

"I can't believe you did it—"

"Thanks."

"I was about to say 'without me.'"

"Oh. Sorry."

"Any regrets?"

"About not including you? No. If things had gone south—and they still could—you can take my place at Sensory."

"I don't want the job." She hears Creed's phone buzz in the background. "You need to get that?"

"I do. Hang on a minute. When he comes back he says, "You'll never guess who just called me!"

"Your baby mama?"

"Rachel Case."

"Let me guess: she gnawed through the straps of her straight jacket and can't wait to see you?"

"Not quite. I didn't tell you earlier, but several weeks ago Ryan Decker and I were invited to check out the facilities at Mount Weather, where they've been holding Rachel for the past two years. I called her and said that Decker had the clout to get her out of there if she played her cards right."

"Why did you care if she got out?"

"I hired her to kill Decker."

"*What?*"

"I offered her ten million dollars to poison the bastard."

"And she *did?*"

"Yup, just now. I wish I could've killed him myself, after what you told me today about Megan Fry. But it's enough that he's dead, and I can't be tied to it."

"Surely they'll suspect Rachel."

"Almost certainly."

"In that case they'll be able to trace the ten million you paid her."

"It won't matter. I put the ten million in her account years ago, long before I ever heard of Ryan Decker."

"What am I missing?"

"Rachel forgot about the account. I just texted her the same information I gave her years ago and she never knew the difference."

"She forgot she already had ten million dollars? She really *is* crazy."

"You never doubted that, did you?"

"Not really." She pauses. "How did you manage to detonate the weapon?"

"I couldn't get Darrell, Joey, and Sadie away from the van long enough to re-configure the bomb, so I wound up putting Joe Penny in the van with Joey and got Sadie and Darrell in the car with Ben Terry. Ben took Sadie and Darrell to the heliport, parked, and pressed the button that activates the fentanyl spray."

"Ben gassed himself?"

"Not really. He and Sadie were up front, Darrell was behind him holding the gun. The spray initiates in the back seat, which gave Ben enough time to open his door and get out. By the time he got to Sadie's door she was unconscious, but hadn't gotten a strong enough dose to put her down for long. Of course, Darrell was out long enough to be tied up and put in a chopper and flown to Sensory Resources. He's in one of our prison cells."

"Does Trudy know?"

"No, so don't tell her."

"So much for marital transparency."

"Don't start with me."

"What happened with Joe Penny?"

"He drove the van to a secluded area, tied Joey to one of the tires, reconfigured the bomb, set a timer, and ran away.

By the time he'd gone three miles, the van blew up. And the rest, as they say, is history."

"What about Joey's cousin?"

"Amer? He's the terrorist I flipped. He was fucking Joey's wife. All they really wanted was each other, so in return for their cooperation, I offered them Witness Protection."

"And they believed you?"

"Right up to the end."

"Any regrets about the mission?"

"Tons. Starting with why it had to be done."

"You can't accept that the president didn't want to appear vulnerable to our enemies and the American people?"

"No. We're *all* vulnerable to our enemies, and only a fool would maintain otherwise. Tell me you understand this."

"I do. I mean, obviously the White House is a complete joke, security-wise. A guy jumps the fence and gets inside the building with a knife and their response is to add a few dogs on the perimeter?" She laughs. "You and I could wipe it out in an afternoon and be home in time for tea."

"My point exactly."

"If you were planning a nuclear attack tonight, why bother launching the drone this morning?"

"If the bomb didn't work, or if I got stopped I knew I'd never get the opportunity to test the drone."

"Still."

"One of the recurring scenarios I've warned the president about is a nuclear strike directed at the White House. Well, we just had one. And though the bomb detonated a safe distance away, it was close enough they might suspect I had prior knowledge of the attack. If for any reason they believe I could have *prevented* the attack, they'd put me away. If they question me about the bomb I'll cop to the drone attack and maintain that's where my focus has been for the past year."

"A classic case of misdirection."

"It should work, because the terrorist angle is authentic. It was an actual terrorist plot that *would* have destroyed the White House and half of D.C. had I not diverted the blast site."

"To be fair, you *could* have prevented it from detonating."

"True, but *they* don't need to know that."

"Sensory should get credit for uncovering the plot. Funding would go through the roof."

"Yeah, but nothing would change. This way's better because the media can ream the Administration and Congress for failing to uncover the plot. When the public demands a plan for major security upgrades, the president can pull out all my recommendations and pretend he's been working on this for a year."

"You think the president will stop living in the White House?"

"No. It's still too powerful a symbol for freedom. But he'll make it less vulnerable."

"How?"

"Everything the public sees above ground will be fortified. More guards, less access. But the real changes will take place underground. Hardened bunkers and other stuff the press won't know about."

"Speaking of bunkers..."

"Yeah?"

"Now that the bomb has gone off I assume all the bigwigs are scrambling to get into Mount Weather. Are you on the invitation list?"

"I don't know. Probably. But I'd never walk peacefully into a place I can't escape."

"If they invite you and you refuse, won't that be a red flag?"

"If they suspect I was involved in the bombing they'll be relieved to know I don't consider the radiation threat serious enough to hide underground."

"What'll you tell them?"

"I'll say I don't want to be locked up in an underground hole with Rachel Case."

She laughs. "You ever think about her, apart from what happened tonight?"

"Every day."

"In a sexual way?"

"No."

"How about Sadie?"

"You mean have I thought about her sexually?"

"No. I mean what's her current status? Is she alive?"

"She is. I ordered her back to your hotel room."

"In that case, do me a small favor?"

"Name it."

"Can you finally get someone to remove my cuffs? I don't want Sadie to see me like this."

"What is it with you and the cuffs?"

"What do you mean?"

"I have no doubt you could have broken free any time you wanted to."

"Yeah, but these are world-class cuffs. I didn't want to break a wrist unless it was an absolute emergency."

"I don't blame you. Wrists are a bitch to heal. Ben's in the parking lot. I'll send him up."

Chapter 2

"I DON'T GET it," Sadie says, eyeing Callie closely as she pours the wine. "Where were you shot?"

Callie takes a sip, then points at the bracelet.

"That's crazy! Was it a real bullet?"

Callie nods. Then says, "I'm sorry you had to deal with the killer alone. I hoped to do a better job of protecting you, but got sidetracked with Joey."

"Don't be silly. You saved my life. You literally took a bullet for me! If you hadn't stepped in for me with Joey I'd be dead. Not to mention...."

"What?"

"Creed originally made a deal with me. Said if I got everyone out of the van for at least an hour he'd let me go. But when it was all over he told me he lied. He said he liked me, but planned to kill me from the very start. Said he couldn't set me free because there were too many people

276

involved. 'Too many loose ends,' he said." She reaches for her glass, takes a sip.

Callie watches her, then says, "And yet here you are."

"Thanks to you."

"What do you mean?"

"Creed told me what you did. He said he owed you a favor from the old days and you asked to cash it in. He said you had a favor coming, one you'd saved up for years—and you wanted to use it to save my life." She looks into Callie's eyes with an expression of gratitude that could so easily be mistaken for warmth it might actually *be* warmth. It's hard for Callie to tell, given Sadie's condition, but when she sees tears in Sadie's eyes she's all but convinced she's experiencing a breakthrough moment. And if true, what could that mean for their future?

Callie shakes the thought out of her head and says, "We need to talk."

"What's wrong?"

"Creed didn't just kidnap Rick, he killed him."

Noting Sadie's face failed to register the slightest change in expression, Callie adds, "Rick's dead. Do you understand?"

"Yes."

Callie frowns. "How does that make you *feel?*"

"Well, he cheated on me."

"That's all you've got to say?"

Sadie shrugs. "What *should* I say?"

They sip some more wine. Callie says, "I'm not going to charge you the eighteen grand."

Sadie cocks her head. "That doesn't sound like you at *all*. What's happened?"

"I saved you from Creed, and from getting raped and shot by Joey, and you gave me the gift of your body, and hours of unmatched pleasure. I consider that an even trade."

"I'm glad to hear that, but I still expect you to honor our agreement."

"What do you mean?"

"I *asked* you to protect me, but I hired you to kill Creed. That was our contract, and the down payment was my body, and the balance was my cash."

"I see."

"You threatened to cut my arms off if I stiffed you for half your fee, so I certainly hope you don't expect to stiff *me* for our entire contract."

"That's why I'm releasing you from the cash portion."

"Sorry. You have to kill him. If you'll recall, my first words on the subject were 'how much would I have to pay you to kill this asshole?'"

"You're putting me in an awkward situation."

Sadie frowns. "Just to be clear, you and I entered into a contract, and I gave you a substantial down payment that was very difficult for me to do. While I appreciate all you've done for me, I'm refusing your settlement. You're either going to have to kill this man, or admit that your word, your contract, means nothing."

"Do you have any feelings for me at all?"

"I don't have feelings for anyone, but I respect you. Especially your courage. Why is that important?"

"I don't know. The way you were looking at me a minute ago, it just seemed like...there might be something more."

"There's not. I'm sorry."

"Pity. Still, you really seemed to enjoy it when we made love. Particularly the second time."

Sadie smiles. "It's nice of you to say that. As you know, it was my first time with a woman, and I tried very hard to come through for you."

"You came through in spades! It was one of the best sexual experiences of my life."

"Thanks for saying so. Of course, the real credit goes to the three sexually frustrated men from my past who eventually taught me how to make the proper movements and sounds at the appropriate times."

"*Excuse* me?"

"It took *years* of practice, believe me!"

"Are you fucking with me right now?"

"No, of course not. But you should have seen me back then. It was hilarious! I used to take notes right there in the bed: *When he touches me here, I moan, when I touch him there, I murmur.* There's a big difference between moans and murmurs, you know."

Callie gives her a look. "You fucking bitch."

"What?"

"You don't have a fucking clue, do you?"

"About what?"

"How badly you insulted me just now."

"What are you *talking* about?"

"What you just said about making love to me: it's the worst thing you could possibly say."

"It *is*?"

"It's a total slap in the face."

"Shit. I'm sorry. I assumed you were seeking complete honesty." She sighs. "My bad. I'm not accustomed to discussing feelings with a female. Can I try again?"

"Who gives a shit?"

"I do. I'm sorry I hurt your feelings. I *can* tell you that the physicality of sex is often pleasurable, and was with you, too."

"Great."

"Especially the second time. The second time gave me a pleasant sensation, and made me realize that doing it with a woman has its advantages."

"Like what?"

"There's not much to clean up afterwards."

"Well that's something, I guess. Does that mean you'd do it again?"

"I might consider it. Wait. You mean *now*?"

"Yes."

"Not willingly."

"Pity."

They sip some more.

Callie says, "I think I could have fallen in love with you."

Sadie says, "Well, you still can. It appears I don't have a husband. If you think I could somehow make you happy we could try living together and see how it goes. But I still expect you to keep your promise."

"To kill Creed?"

"Yes."

"Why is that so important to you?"

"He broke into my home and frightened me. Killed my husband. Killed my neighbor. Forced me to kill a stranger. Terrorized me, and ran me out of town, and put me in harm's way numerous times. Caused me to have unwanted sex with a murderous lesbian—no offense—and to lose my life's savings. You and I entered into a contract, Callie. Creed has to die, and you have to kill him."

"Kiss me?" Callie says.

"No."

"Why not?"

"I don't feel like it."

"How *do* you feel?"

"Tired. Exhausted."

"Makes sense. You know you're dying, right?"

"What do you mean?"

"I poisoned your wine."

Chapter 3

Next Day...

"ANY FALLOUT FROM Homeland?" Callie asks.

"Not yet," Creed says. "The top guns are still hiding out at Mount Weather."

"Pussies."

Creed laughs.

They're on the phone, trying to arrange a visit that's been rendered problematic due to the million snakes covering Creed's lawn, surrounding his estate.

"How's Darrell?" Callie says.

"Unhappy."

"I'm surprised you didn't kill him."

"I promised Trudy I wouldn't."

"You told her?"

"I was influenced by your comment, about marital transparency."

"That was a mistake. Trudy's *way* too soft."

"I thought so too, till she gave me the green light to torture him."

"No shit?" Callie laughs. "I'm impressed. By the way, I've been watching the news."

"The bombing or the snakes?"

"Both. I actually think the public's more interested in the snakes than the nuclear attack."

"It's an oddity. Celebrities are calling us nonstop, trying to arrange photo ops to be released whenever their publicists decide which side of the issue they should support."

"What're their choices?"

"Are the snakes pro-war or anti-war? Are they victims or predators? Are any of them endangered? Do they require medical treatment? If so, is the government doing all they can to solve their plight?"

"What's Trudy saying?"

"She thinks the danger hasn't passed," Creed says.

"What danger?"

"She doesn't know, but thinks it might have something to do with Rose wanting to come take the baby. Like you, Trudy talked about all the coincidences and said they all make sense if you start with the premise that Rose coordinated it."

"I doubt Rose is afraid of snakes."

"I agree. Especially since she claims to speak their language."

"Snakes have a language?"

"According to Trudy and Rose."

283

Callie laughs. "Well, I still want to come and return the bracelet and give her that hug she wanted."

"It'll mean the world to her. And me."

"It's the least I can do. I mean, she may or may not have saved my life, but she certainly saved my hand."

"I'll send the chopper for you. How long can you stay?"

"Is Trudy planning to make persimmon pudding?"

"If you wish."

"Tell her I'll stay till it runs out."

"That'll make her happy. By the way, thanks for coming through with Sadie."

"It was one of the hardest jobs I've ever done."

"Really? How come?"

"She was a helluva woman."

"How so?"

"She had a mental condition so severe you'd expect her to have been institutionalized since childhood. But she learned to live with it so well she actually carved out a semi-normal life, complete with husband, friends, a house, a car she could actually drive...she was *heroic*, Donovan. And after achieving all that, through no fault of her own, you plucked her out of her universe yesterday morning, terrorized her, turned her into a killer, and dismantled her life, piece by piece, till there was nothing left but the clothes on her back and the pulse in her neck. And now even that's gone."

"Sorry I asked. Where should I send the chopper?"

Callie sighs. "You know Cartwright Aviation, at Bowman Municipal?"

"No, but our pilot will."

"Tell him I'll meet him there in thirty minutes."

"The snakes have been acting up all morning. Maybe you'd better give me an hour, just in case."

"No rush, get him there when you can. I'll be waiting."

"See you soon."

"You too."

Chapter 4

NOW, HOVERING OVER Creed's estate, the full magnitude of the snake issue is overwhelming. Snakes of every type have encircled his home and grounds, and cover every square inch of land for a full mile. A dozen helicopters are buzzing the estate, taking aerial photos and videos. At the outermost edge in every direction, Callie can see news trucks and reporters covering the story, interviewing some of the hundreds of scientists, misfits, and crazy people who have come from all corners of the earth to try to make sense out of the strange migration. The popular theory? The snake population near Washington, D.C. somehow sensed the impending nuclear attack and migrated toward the western part of the state. When the bomb went off, the snakes became confused and remained where they were. Experts fear they'll die soon and will create a major health hazard.

The chopper lands, and to Callie's surprise, the snakes swarm it. The biggest ones are striking the cockpit glass repeatedly, as if trying to break it.

On the phone with Creed, she says, "Are you watching this?"

"I am. It's crazy. The chopper's completely covered. Don't try to get out. I don't want to scare you, but a lot of them are poisonous."

"What should I do?"

"Wait for Trudy."

"What can *she* do?"

"They typically make a path for her."

"It better be a wide path!"

"Give us a few minutes. We'll see what we can do."

Chapter 5

IT TOOK THIRTY minutes, but Trudy finally drove the snakes from the chopper and somehow managed to keep them at bay long enough for Callie and the pilot to get to the house safely. Now, in the grand hallway, Trudy says, "I'm so sorry about the snakes."

"They were attacking the *chopper!*" Callie says. "I've never seen anything like it!"

"Well, you're safe now." She looks at Creed, then back at Callie and says, "Donovan said if I made you a batch of persimmon puddin' you might give me that hug I asked for."

Callie takes a deep breath, then holds her arms open like she's about to catch a bridal bouquet she doesn't want. Trudy moves to her quickly, as if worried Callie might change her mind.

They hug, and Trudy holds her tightly. Then steps back and says, "I know that didn't come easy. I'm thankful."

Callie removes her bracelet and hands it to Trudy.

"I didn't believe you at the time," she says, "but I'm glad I wore it. Thank you."

Trudy says, "You should give it to someone who needs it more."

"It belongs to you."

Trudy laughs. "It'll come back to me someday. It always does."

"Well...I do know someone who might benefit from it, if you're serious."

She says, "I am. In fact, I *insist* you give it to that person!"

"Very well." Callie puts the bracelet back on, opens her handbag and says, "I brought you some wine."

Chapter 6

"WHY THANK YOU!" Trudy says. She accepts the bottle, walks over to Creed, hands it to him. He stares at Trudy strangely, blinks a couple of times.

"Are you okay?" Trudy asks.

"Yes, of course," Creed says. "It's just—I don't know. I'm picking up some sort of scent."

Trudy cocks her head. "That's an odd thing to say."

Callie says, "It's probably my perfume. From when we hugged."

"I know your perfume," Creed says. "This is sweeter."

"It's something new. I found it among Sadie Sharp's things."

Creed gives her a stern look.

Trudy winks. "Am I allowed to ask who that is?"

"I'm afraid it's a long story with a sad ending," Creed says. "Sadie was a friend of Callie's. She passed away recently."

"Oh, I'm so sorry!" Trudy says. "I hadn't heard!"

"She was more of an acquaintance than friend," Callie corrects. "But I thought I'd honor her today by wearing her scent."

"Good for you!" Trudy says. She gathers a handful of hair and sweeps it toward her nose. "I like the scent!" she says. Then sidles up to Creed so he can smell it. He does, and coughs.

"Let's open the wine," Callie says.

"Creed stares at her a long time before saying, "I don't remember you being so fond of wine at this time of day."

Trudy shows him a frown and says, "I'd love to try it."

He shrugs. "I'll open it in the den and be right back."

"We'll come with you," Trudy says.

"No need," Creed says. "I should let it breathe a few minutes. Have a seat, ladies. I'll be right back."

He leaves the room. Trudy says, "I'm so sorry. Everyone's on edge about the snakes. Even Donovan, it appears. And what an awful reception we gave *you!* You must have been terrified!"

"I'm not terrified of anything," Callie sniffs.

"Oh, I didn't mean to imply—"

"It's okay. I know what you meant. Where's the baby?"

Trudy sighs. "I put her in the bedroom and closed the door."

"Is she still hissing?"

"No."

"Then what's wrong?"

"I hate to speak ill of Hawley, but she threw a God-awful fit just before you arrived. I swear, I don't know what came *over* that girl! I reckon it'll do her good to be alone for a spell."

"Well, I'm sure she'll be fine soon. Donovan says she's the best baby ever."

"Oh, she *is*! She's *never* like this."

"I'd love to see her again, when you release her from time out. Speaking of prisoners, have you had the opportunity to spend much time with Megan Fry?"

Trudy frowns. "I'm afraid she's been a rather unpleasant guest."

"How so?"

"She hates us."

"How's that possible?"

"I know, right?"

Callie laughs. "Will you do me a favor?"

"Of course! Name it!"

"Would you have Anson fetch her?"

Trudy bites her lip. "Fetch Megan?"

"Yes."

"I should probably ask Donovan."

"It'll be all right. I have a special connection with her. I guarantee she'll be nice to you."

Trudy gives her a look. "You're not going to...uh..."

"No, of course not. Why, has she *said* something?"

"Actually, she told us terrible things about you."

"Like what?"

"Oh, I couldn't say."

"Why not?"

"Beatin' a dead horse don't make it taste better."

"I have no idea what that means, but I'd really like to see her. Just for a minute. I have a very important question to ask her."

"Well...."

"It'll be okay. I promise."

Trudy presses a button on the side of her watch and says, "Anson? Could you bring Megan to the grand hallway? ...Yes....It'll be okay..." She looks at Callie, smiles, rolls her eyes. "No, you don't have to check with Mr. Creed....Yes, I'm sure. Thank you."

Moments later, a clearly uncomfortable Anson leads a clearly furious Megan into the room. She's wearing handcuffs and has a red plastic ball in her mouth that's held in place with a black strap that circles her head.

"Hello, Megan," Callie says.

Megan's eyes grow large. Her posture instantly goes from angry to submissive. Trudy says, "Megan? Please try to be civil. Callie has something very important to ask you." She looks at Callie and says, "Go ahead."

Callie says, "Megan, I need your expertise. I want you to walk with us into the den, examine Donovan Creed's body, and tell me if he's clinically dead."

Chapter 7

AFTER REMOVING A gun from her handbag and pointing it at Anson; after assuring Trudy this wasn't some sort of
sick joke; after removing Megan's gag ball and handcuffs and
leading them all into the den; after explaining to Trudy that
it's actually hurting Creed's chances of surviving when she
hugs his body, screaming and crying...she tells Megan:
"During the months Creed and I dated, I collected numerous samples of his DNA and had it analyzed and sequenced
by a top microbiologist, who helped me develop a gene-
specific poison that's safe for anyone on the planet except
Donovan Creed. Before entering your home, Trudy, I
sprayed it on my hair, knowing you wanted to hug me.
Through simple transference and a trusting heart, you poisoned your husband. I distracted him with the wine, to
throw him off his game. So Megan, if you'll do the honors?
Quickly please, I haven't got all day."

Megan drops to the floor, calls Creed's name loudly, taps his shoulders forcefully. Then presses her knuckles on his sternum. Then pokes him.

Creed makes a sound and expels some air through his nose and throat.

"Thank God!" Trudy shouts.

"Actually, it's a sign of death," Megan says. "People who are not dead but unconscious never make sounds when poked. Conversely, dead people always do."

Trudy grabs her head with both hands and moans, "Please God. Please God. Please don't let him die." It's more of a chant, though, and her words have a resignation about them.

Meanwhile, Megan's shaking him, checking his pulse and his breathing.

"Get me a mirror or spoon," she says. "Now!"

Trudy jumps to her feet, runs to the bar, flings the top drawer open, grabs a spoon, gives it to Megan. "What can I do?" Trudy says.

"You got a flashlight?"

"If it's in the room," Callie says. "No one leaves the room."

"There's a flashlight app on my phone," Trudy says.

"That'll work," Megan says. She holds the back of the spoon under Creed's nose. "Just so you know, I'm looking for steam. If the spoon steams up, he's absolutely alive."

Trudy leans in close, stares closely at the spoon for fifteen seconds, but sees no steam, which launches her into a crying fit. "Oh, God!" she screams. "Oh, God!" She turns to Callie. "What have you done?"

"I contracted to kill him," Callie says. "I had to fulfill the contract."

Trudy turns her focus back on her husband. "Oh, God! Oh, please God, no! *NO!*"

Megan stares carefully into his eyes. Then says, "I'm ready to try the flashlight/pupil test." Trudy holds the flashlight app to Creed's eyes, but it yields nothing. Finally, Megan says, "Get me some alcohol."

"What kind?" Trudy says. "Rubbing or liquor?"

"Any kind of liquor. Whatever's open. And a napkin."

Trudy grabs a bottle of bourbon and a paper napkin from the bar, hands it to Megan. She pours some bourbon on the napkin and holds it under Creed's nose. After a moment, she looks at her watch, turns to Callie and says, "Based on everything that can be measured outside an intensive care environment, I can say with reasonable certainty he's dead."

Callie says, "Thanks, Megan. From the first day we trained together, Donovan always said one of us would eventually kill the other. I think we both assumed it would be him killing me. But the combination of Kimberly's death and Trudy's love threw him off his game."

Trudy seems oblivious to Callie's words. She's on her knees, rocking back and forth, whispering "*Do* something, Donovan. *Do* something!"

Callie, watching the tears spill from Trudy's eyes, says, "This is beyond the realm of magic, Trudy; beyond backwoods potions, remedies, and elixirs. It's not something your miracle bracelet can prevent."

Trudy suddenly looks up and says, "Anson!"

"Yes Miss?"

"Start counting!"

"*What?*"

"Stand over him and count to ten. Like a referee! Start counting, Anson! He'll get up, I promise! *No* one counts Donovan Creed out! No one!"

Anson says, "Miss...I'm so sorry...he's gone."

No one looks at Callie's face, or they'd see the smallest tear falling from her eye. She says, "Megan, I know there's a technical difference between death and clinical death. Can you review it for me? I don't want there to be any doubt about Creed's condition."

"Clinical death is the final physical state before legal death," Megan says. "It's the cessation of breathing and blood circulation, both of which are necessary to sustain human life."

"Would you say Creed is clinically dead?"

"Yes, though we don't have the proper medical equipment to confirm it."

"But that's the same reason it's less likely he could be resuscitated, correct?"

"Without the proper equipment, outside a hospital environment, it would be impossible to resuscitate him."

"Thank you. And how long can a person's brain survive after being pronounced clinically dead?"

"All measurable brain activity ceases within forty seconds."

"And we're past that now?"

"Yes."

"And yet I've heard of cases where people were pronounced dead but were resuscitated minutes later and survived."

"That won't happen here. Certain tissues and organs can survive clinical death for minutes, even hours, but not the brain. Without special treatment, full recovery of the brain beyond three minutes is virtually impossible."

"There's that word again, 'virtually.' At what point does it become completely, totally, one hundred percent impossible for Creed to come back to life?"

"The five minute mark. But that only applies if he were in an advanced care facility, with a team of specialists."

"In this setting, what do you consider the point of no return?"

"Forty seconds."

"And where are we currently?"

Megan checks her watch. "We just passed the two minute mark."

"Is there any possible way to resuscitate him at this point?"

"No."

Trudy suddenly comes to life and shouts, "*Hawley!*" She jumps to her feet, starts running toward the door.

Callie shouts, "If you take another step, I'll shoot."

"Go ahead," Trudy says, "But you'll have to deal with Hawley's wrath."

"I'll shoot *him*, not you," she says, pointing the gun at Creed's heart.

Trudy stops in her tracks, takes a deep breath; then whispers the only word she knows will save the day. It's the word she dreads uttering more than any other, the word that could bring her entire world crashing down around her ears.

Callie says, "Sorry, I didn't catch that. What did you just say?"

"I said 'Rose.'"

"Fuck."

Chapter 8

A FULL THIRTY seconds pass as everyone looks around the room, nervously.

Trudy's stunned. She closes her eyes, concentrates harder. Then screams, "ROSE!"

Callie waits another moment before saying, "For the briefest moment, I actually thought she'd materialize! Not that it matters." She places a syringe in Megan's hand and says, "Inject this into Donovan's thigh, please."

"What is it?"

"The antidote."

Trudy says, "There's an *antidote?*"

"Of *course* there is!" Callie says. "You didn't think I'd actually let him die *permanently*, did you? I *love* this bastard!"

A few tense minutes later, as Creed starts coming to, Callie says, "I think he'll be okay."

"What he'll be," Trudy says, "is mad as hell."

"I agree. Perhaps I should leave before he regains his strength."

"Really? Just how do you plan to avoid the snakes?"

"I assumed you'd clear the way for me."

"Think again, bitch."

Callie points the gun at Creed. "I could kill him for real."

"You could, but you won't."

"She might," Anson says.

"Call your pilot," Callie says. "I won't ask you a second time."

Trudy looks at Anson.

He nods.

She says, "I welcomed you into my home, Callie. Trusted you. Saved your hand from gettin' blown off. Not to mention Donovan has *always* been there for you. And *this* is how you repay us?"

"It sounds worse than it is. Donovan will understand. He knows I always fulfill my contracts. He'll forgive me."

"If you believe that, tell him yourself."

"He'll forgive me...in *time*," Callie amends. "He always does."

"I think maybe you stretched the taffy a little too thin this time."

"He'll be pissed, but I guarantee he'll forgive me. And you know why?"

"I'd love to hear it."

"Because I now owe *him* a favor. And whatever he makes me do to square things up will be ten times worse than what I just put him through."

It takes a few minutes, but Creed works his way to a sitting position. He tries to speak, but nothing comes out. He clears his throat, tries again. Finally says, "Trudy?"

"Yes?"

"I love all this attention but...could you please not lean over me?"

"What do you mean? What's wrong?"

"Uh...your *hair*?"

"Omigod! I'm so *sorry!*"

She rushes twenty steps away, as does Callie.

Creed says, "Callie's right. I *do* understand, and I *do* forgive her, and she *does* owe me a favor." He pauses, then adds, "And I already have a plan for cashing in that favor."

"Fuck," Callie says.

Trudy grabs a hand towel from the bar, wraps it tightly around her hair, runs back to her husband, throws her arms around him, kisses him twenty times in two seconds.

Callie looks at Megan and frowns. "You believe this shit? I think I'm gonna vomit."

Megan says, "You people are crazy. In every possible way."

THE END

Continue reading for bonus material...

Outtakes from *This Means War!*

Pre-publication Argument between Author, John Locke, and Character, Trudy Lake

John Locke, writing:

SHE WAS YOUNG, *the room was cold; her nipples were as puckered as a grandmother's kiss. She moved beneath me gracefully, with a tenderness only a gifted poet could describe. We made love slowly, with reverence, by candlelight. Afterward—*

"Bullshit!"

I jump at the sound, see Trudy looking over my shoulder. "What's wrong?"

"No way! Delete that this *instant!*"

"Delete what?"

"That whole business about my nipples. Eew!"

"It's a great line!" I say. "It's been in my head for over a year."

"It's disgustin'. And everyone who buys your book is gonna want to see if it's true. I'll be asked to lift my shirt every time I turn around."

"You're being silly. First of all, no one's going to buy this book."

Trudy frowns. "They better not. But you've got an editor, right? And a publisher? I don't want *them* thinkin' I've got granny nipples, either. And I don't, by the way, so tell me."

"Tell you what?"

"What made you *write* that? Where'd you *hear* it?"

"I didn't hear it anywhere."

"You mean you just...what, made it *up?*"

"That's right. I'm an author. I come up with a good line, I use it. Sue me."

"I'll sure as hell sue you if you go around tellin' the world I've got granny nipples!"

"I never said you had granny nipples. I said they were puckered from the cold."

"I could probably sue you for *that.*"

"You'd have to prove it."

"What?"

"If you sue me, you'll have to prove in court your nipples weren't as puckered as a grandmother's kiss on the day I'm writing about."

"That day ain't even *happened* yet."

"True. I'm getting ahead of myself."

"That's unusual for you, isn't it? Aren't you always *behind* in your writin'? How many times have you promised your next book would be a Donovan Creed or Emmett Love?"

"This *is* a Donovan Creed book."

"Are you sure?"

"Positive. Why?"

"Based on the title, I figured it was about me. You know, *Another Man, Another Chance*? I was with Gideon, now I'm with Creed."

"That's the old title. I changed it to *This Means War!*"

She rolls her eyes. "That's the worst title I ever heard for a romance novel."

"It's a thriller."

"Big mistake. People are buyin' romance novels. They want to see me and Donovan fall in love."

"You and Creed? In love?"

"Of course! Why else would he be thinkin' thoughts about my nipples and such?"

"Because he's Creed!"

"After all this time can you really give him so little credit? He knows I'm not like the others. He can see I'm his last chance for true love."

"So?"

"All I'm sayin', if I'm in your book, I expect a certain amount of accuracy."

I sigh.

"It's the least you can do," she says.

"Fine. How should I describe your nipples?"

"You shouldn't describe 'em at *all*. And while we're on the subject, you think maybe your sales would improve if you toned down all the sex and nasty parts?"

"No."

"Lively."

"Excuse me?"

"If you *have* to describe 'em, say they're lively."

"Your nipples are *lively?*"

"That's right."

"That doesn't make sense."

"Oh, so suddenly your writin' has to make *sense?*"

Donovan Creed, Pre-publication, Section 4, Chapter 6:

I FIND ANSON on the front porch, but notice Trudy on the grounds, so I wave him off and approach her. As I close the distance between us I ask, "What's your fascination with dog shit?"

Trudy gives me a look. "Jumpin' the gun, are we?"

"What do you mean?"

She laughs. "Want me to say my line anyway?"

I nod.

She shrugs. "Do you always start conversations this way?"

"Only when I'm told my guests are...wait. Where's the dog shit?"

"I haven't picked it up yet."

I look on the ground.

No dog shit.

I look around the area where we're walking.

Same thing.

No dog shit.

I turn back toward the front door and yell, "Anson? Where's the dog shit?"

He gives the yard a quick glance. "Sorry, sir!"

Trudy laughs.

I shake my head. "This book has barely started and it's already a cluster-fuck."

Trudy Lake / Donovan Creed:

"WE'RE LONG-LIVED," Trudy says.

"Who is?"

"My family. Most of my kinfolk made it well past a hundred."

"But your mom?"

"That don't count. She was hung to death."

"Seriously?"

She nods.

"How long did it take?"

Trudy does a double-take. "*Excuse* me?"

"Uh..."

"That's inappropriate, Donovan, even for you. Jesus!" She reaches in her pocket. "Here's a nickel. Go tell John to write you a better response."

Trudy Lake
(*reviewing the galley proof*):

"HER ASS LOOKS like two Peterbilts fighting for a *parking* spot?"

I say, "That's supposed to be a statement. Not a question."

"I doubt your readers know what a Peterbilt is."

"My publisher does."

"Claudia Jackson?"

"Yup. She got hit by one just last week."

"Was she walkin' or drivin' at the time?"

"Driving. But it's okay. She's fine."

"Tell her I'm glad she survived. But I'm still not sayin' that line in your novel."

"Why not?"

"I don't like criticizin' people's looks."

"It's a funny line."

"Not to the lady with the big butt."

"Look. First of all, it's fiction. Second, the lady in the book, Ingrid, was putting you down. She was making fun of you."

"That don't make it right to talk about her butt. She's probably real sensitive about it."

I sigh. "It's not like you *started* it. Look. I just want the readers to know you're willing to stick up for yourself. All I'm saying, if someone throws dirt at you, it's okay to throw it back."

"My granny says when you throw dirt, you lose ground."

"Yeah, but that's..."

"Yeah?"

"Actually, that's quite profound."

"Bet you wish you'd said it."

"I do, actually."

"It's an old sayin'."

"You're sure about that?"

"Granny used to say it every time she washed our mouths out with soap." Trudy pauses, recalling the memory. Then says, "John?"

"Yeah?"

"You want to write me true, don't you?"

"Of course."

"Then you should delete the line altogether. And while you're at it, delete Ingrid."

"Why?"

"She don't move the plot forward, and she ain't funny. Ain't those the only two rules you follow in your writin'?"

"I'm not married to the line. I could be persuaded to eliminate the entire scene, as well as Ingrid's character."

"You could?"

"If you'll agree to the Mammoth Cave line."

Trudy frowns. "The hotdog/Mammoth cave line?"

I nod.

"How come I can't just say somethin' normal?"

"Because I don't write normal books. You of all people should know that! And anyway, it's a great line."

She wrinkles her nose. "You think?"

"It's hilarious. Trust me: when they read the hotdog/Mammoth Cave line, they'll laugh out loud."

"What if your readers think I'm bein' serious when I say it?"

"Everyone knows you've got a great heart, Trudy. They'll know I made you say it. They'll know it was just me, being silly. Try it."

"What, you mean now?"

"Why not?"

She takes a deep breath, says, "I can't picture you fuckin' Rachel. Havin' sex with her would be like heavin' a hotdog into Mammoth Cave."

She gives me a look. "That's funny to you?"

I can barely hear her over my laughter. "Yeah," I say, finally. "It's hilarious."

"Well I ain't sayin' it."

"Fine. I'll give it to Callie. But don't come back to me later complaining I never give you the good stuff."

Bonus Scenes

Note from John Locke:

THOSE FAMILIAR WITH my work are aware that when I finish the first draft of my novels, I check the word count, then go back and trim five to ten percent of the book to make it read faster. Then I send the manuscript to several key readers and ask them to check for errors and highlight the parts they like and don't like, paying special attention to any portion they felt was too wordy. I also ask for their overall impressions of the work. After making the corrections I go back and see if there are any parts I can trim or eliminate to speed the book along for the reader. My goal is that every scene I write will advance the plot, or cause the reader to react. Usually that means a smile or laugh.

That said, there are numerous scenes, and many thousands of words left over that never make it into each of my books. Over the years I'm sure more than a hundred readers have asked me to include some of these cutting-floor sections in the next book, and I've never done it for various reasons. One is I don't want readers to think I'm padding my word count, as I've been criticized numerous times for simply including the first chapter or two of the next book in a given series!

This time I decided to add a few of the deleted scenes because this particular novel challenged me more than any of my others. Book #11 in the Creed saga ended with Creed in a very dark place. When I started writing Book #11 I quickly realized I had painted myself into a bit of a corner, as it's impossible for a man to be happy, funny, and light-hearted after his daughter has just been killed. Add to that Creed's failed relationship with Callie, and you've got a difficult chore to get this man back to where we all like him. The problem: time has to pass before he's ready to move on with his life. And that time is necessarily filled with self-doubt, gloominess, and despair.

But readers don't want to spend hours—or even minutes—with a gloomy Creed.

So that was a big challenge.

Some of you will read *This Means War!* and think I left too much in here about Creed and Trudy's courtship. Others will say I didn't include enough. I can tell you, it's a tough call. So this time I'll cater to the 100-plus who asked for some deleted scenes, and take my lumps if this bonus material offends you.

I chopped more than 10,000 words from this novel, and the following are just a few of the short scenes that didn't make it into the finished product.

One last thing: for those who complain my novels are often shorter than the books they usually read I can honestly tell you it's a lot harder to trim a novel down than it is to add a lot of filler. When I submitted *Saving Rachel* to a well-respected editor he said he could get it published by a major publishing house if I added 20,000 words of filler. I asked him what type of filler did he have in mind. "Descriptive elements," he said. Details of characters' looks, clothing, and manner. Details about the restaurants, clubs, homes, and businesses they visit. Details about the lighting. The temperature. The weather. I told him that adding all those things would slow the pace of the book to a crawl. "Readers expect those elements," he said. "If you leave them out they'll think you don't know how to write."

"I'll take my chances," I said, believing there had to be a whole audience out there who reads books the way I do, meaning they skip over most of the descriptive elements to get to the action and fun stuff.

"What about flashbacks?" he said. "*Saving Rachel* is the third book of the series. You could add thousands of words just re-hashing the characters' back stories."

I tried to explain that the original version of *Saving Rachel* had 7,000 more words, but I trimmed them down to speed up the reading. I also tried to explain what I just told you: that it's harder to cut words than to add them, and gave this example:

A famous speaker was asked, "How much preparation time does it take to give a good speech?" He answered, "It depends on how long you want the speech to be. If you want five minutes, it'll take me a week. If you want a fifteen minute speech, I'll need two days. If you want an hour-long speech, I'm ready right now."

So anyway, here are a few of the numerous scenes I deleted. I hope you don't come away thinking I included them, or this explanation, because I was trying to build my word count!

Bonus Scene #1: The Angel's Share

Trudy & Creed:

"ARE YOUR PARENTS alive, Mr. Creed?"

"No."

"Oh," Trudy says. "I'm sorry."

"Kids always bitch about their parents," I say. "What they don't realize, parents are a luxury. No one looks at it that way until they're gone. When you're the only orphan in the neighborhood you grow up wondering if the reason God failed to save your parents is because He wanted to punish you."

"That's so sad! Of *course* it's not your fault. Wait. *Was* it your fault?"

I frown. "No. How about *your* parents?"

"Mom didn't make it, but my father's still walkin' among us."

"Well, that's good."

"You wouldn't say that if you knew him."

I smile for reasons I can't explain. Maybe it's because I like the way Trudy has definite feelings about people and isn't afraid to express them, even to strangers. Of course, I know more about her family than I'm letting on, having checked her out thoroughly before agreeing to let her stay here. For example, I know her father's a deputy sheriff in a Western Kentucky town that's smaller than the tract of land my house sits on. He's also a drug dealer and alleged murderer who served time for molesting Trudy's sister. Bad as he is, most of her kinfolk are worse! Take Renee Williams: Trudy doesn't know whether Renee Williams is her cousin, sister, stepsister, or all the above, but what's not in question is the fact that Renee, a 30-year-old school teacher, admitted to murdering at least two people and is widely considered to be bat shit crazy.

I wonder what sort of people *aren't* approved to sheriff or teach school in Trudy's home town!

Trudy's personal history is no less sketchy. For one thing she's technically married—to her brother, no less!—and the child she brought with her—Hawley—isn't hers. She was recently living with Dr. Gideon Box in his New York City apartment, though I'm still trying to decipher their relationship. My guess is he found her in Kentucky several months ago, talked her into moving to Manhattan, and hoped to turn her into a kept woman. I don't know if he kicked her out or if she fled. Maybe she didn't take to the lifestyle, or ran away to punish him or test their relationship. Or maybe she turned out to be more than the good doctor could handle. But somewhere along the way Trudy borrowed or stole a baby.

Darrel, Trudy's husband/brother, is a piece of work in his own right. His history of violence includes murder, bestiality, and kidnapping. He also makes and sells moonshine and crystal meth; sells illegal assault weapons; and is a tireless forger, blackmailer, arsonist, and defrauder of insurance companies.

Trudy, for all the bad influences, has never been arrested. Though only 18 years old (or 17, 19, 20, or 21), she's worked in restaurants and volunteered at the county hospital since the age of eight (or 7, 9, 10, or 11). She was the homecoming queen of her high school, where she graduated as valedictorian, with a perfect 4.0 grade-point average. She was also voted by her classmates as "Most Popular," "Prettiest Smile," "Smartest," and "Most Likely to Run Away from Home."

Maybe she ran away to New York City with Dr. Box, created a home there, and ran away from it. Maybe she can't stay put. Makes me wonder how long she'll stay here.

"We're long-lived," Trudy says.

"Who is?"

"My family. I come from a line of long-lived people. Most of my kinfolk make it well past a hundred."

"But your mom?"

"That don't count. She was hung to death."

I arch an eyebrow. *There's* a story my investigators didn't uncover, and one I'd like to hear more about, but one of the very few things I've learned about women is you have to let them reveal their stories and secrets in their own way, in their own time. If you're patient, a woman will tell you everything. *Far* more than you want to know! It's their nature to share either too little or too much. But to get the secrets, you can't prod or push. The trick is to act interested, but not desperate, to hear them.

I'm at the interested stage, so instead of asking about her mom's hanging, I ask, "To what do you attribute your family's longevity?"

Trudy gives me a funny look, then says, "We keep the Angel's Share."

"I'm familiar with the term," I say, "But only in the context of whiskey evaporation."

She smiles. "Same thing, except with people."

I say nothing, hoping she'll reward me with an explanation.

She does: "When whiskey's distilled, a certain amount of the batch is lost to evaporation. People say it goes straight to heaven."

"The Angel's Share."

"That's right, and people are the same way. When most people fall in love, they're happy all the time. Everything about the relationship's a joy. When they get married, it's the fulfillment of their life's dream. They're so excited! When they get a new friend, they love everything about that person, and want to know all there is to know about 'em. When they get a new job, they spend an hour gettin' ready that first day. They show up early, stay late, give it their full attention. But over time, whether it's romance, marriage, friendships, or work, most people take things for granted. Their joy, enthusiasm, and wonder evaporate straight to heaven. They've still got their lover, spouse, friends, or job, but those things don't mean what they once did."

"And your family?"

"We're selfish. We keep the Angel's Share of our happiness for ourselves. Don't get me wrong, me and my kinfolk do lots of wrong-minded things, but we do 'em enthusiastically. If we get a friend we keep a friend. If we love, we tend to keep lovin'. Most of my kinfolk don't hold legitimate jobs, but they're all thankful for the work they have, and they work hard. They always give their best days' work. Them that don't keep a joyful, thankful attitude durin' the rough patches are sendin' all them good thoughts heavenward. And every time you allow some of your wonder and excitement to evaporate, there's less for you to enjoy down here. Over time, you get suspicious and mean, and it takes more and more to trigger your feelin's of wonder. You know what I believe?"

"Tell me."

"I believe we're all born with a certain amount of wonder and fascination, but if we let too much of it evaporate to heaven there ain't much left to live for past a certain age."

I tell her: "No couple can maintain that lover's high over time."

She looks surprised. "Who told you that?"

"It's just common sense."

"It's common, maybe, but that don't mean it makes sense. Not to me, anyway."

"Are you claiming your feelings of love have never diminished over time?"

"Nope. But I'm always conscious of 'em, and that makes me appreciate 'em more than most folks. Then again, I've not found my true love yet."

"Are you looking for him?"

She laughs. "I don't go out shakin' bushes or trees, if that's what you mean. But I'm open to what the universe might send my way."

"And if the universe sends your true love?"

"It won't amount to a hill of beans unless I'm *his* true love, too."

"And if you are?"

"Then we'll keep the angel's share of that love for ourselves."

"And if your true love grows bored?"

"That won't happen if I'm doin' my job right. And I will."

"That *sounds* good, but I wonder if it's true."

"You'd best believe my true love won't have the opportunity to lose interest in me!" she says, emphatically.

"What're you going to do, hogtie him?"

She winks. "I might could, if he were to ask kindly."

Bonus Scene #2: Vegetable Soup

Trudy & Creed:

"CAN I COOK for you sometime?" Trudy says.

"There's no need. We have a full-time professional chef."

"I know. And he's super qualified and fancy-taught. But home cookin' is somethin' different. It's a skill handed down from generation to generation, ever since...well, forever. It's the way I bonded with my mom and the way she bonded with hers, goin' all the way back to the time cookin' was invented. It's part of my heritage, and one I'd like to teach Hawley, when she's old enough."

"Well..."

"It'd be a shame to lose all them generations of cookin' ideas and flavors just 'cause you can pay someone else to do it. And though he's way more skilled than me, I can bring a different style of love to the table, since my learnin' came from a whole different place and time."

"Are you asking me to fire my chef?"

"No, of *course* not! I ain't even proved myself yet! I'm just askin' if you'd consider givin' him a day off once a week."

I frown. "What would you cook?"

"Pretty much anything you like, long as it's comfort food. I can start with somethin' universal, like vegetable soup."

"Oh."

"What's wrong?"

"When you said comfort food I was hoping for something a bit more substantial."

She says, "You ain't even tasted my vegetable soup and you're already *complainin'*?"

"I'm more a meat-and-potatoes sort of guy."

"Good to hear, 'cause I excel at critter meat. But don't overlook vegetables. They're our friends."

I smile. "If they're your friends, why kill them?"

She gives me a look. "Some people might ask *you* the same question." Before I have time to respond she adds, "People and vegetables have a special relationship. We plant 'em, *feed* 'em, and then they feed us. Without us, they wouldn't be here. Without them, *we* wouldn't be here."

"Are you claiming people invented vegetables?"

"No, but I think we perfected plantin' and growin' 'em. I took the liberty of goin' through your pantry and you know what my first question is?"

"I can't imagine."

"Where's your parsley?"

"Parsley?" I shake my head. "I'm not a big fan. I doubt we have any."

"That can't be true. Your chef would insist on it."

"My chef knows not to insist on anything."

She gives me a look. "I might have to rethink cookin' for you."

"Why?"

"I might insist on stuff."

I smile. "I might like that, coming from you."

"What you *might* like is parsley in your soup."

"I doubt that."

"Would you take a blanket to a picnic?"

"Of course."

"Parsley's like a blanket for your vegetable soup."

"That sounds a bit hyperbolic, don't you think?"

"I don't know what that means, but learned a long time ago to never agree with a man if his question includes a word I don't know."

I shake my head. "Hyperbolic simply means—"

She holds up her hand up to stop me. "I'll look it up."

"You don't trust my explanation?"

"Not when it comes to fancy words."

"Why not?"

She pauses. "You know what cunilingus means?"

I do a double take. "Yes, of course."

"Well, I do too, but once upon a time I didn't. So when my uncle approached me on the subject I asked my mom what it meant, and she said, 'Do I look like Mr. Evans to you?' And I said, 'No ma'am—"

"Who's Mr. Evans?"

"My school teacher at the time. Anyway, she said, 'You should go ask Mr. Evans! But don't ask in front of everyone, in case it's somethin' that'll make you look stupid for not knowin'.' I said, 'How should I ask him what cunnilingus means?' She said, 'Tell him you'd like to meet him for a couple minutes after school in private. When you get there, ask him what he knows about cunnilingus.'"

I stare at her a long time before responding. Then say, "I look forward to trying your soup."

"Good. Where's your cabbage?"

"What cabbage?"

"Don't even *tell* me you don't like cabbage!"

I shrug.

"Mr. Creed, you're about to experience a whole new level of joy."

"You think?"

"You're standing at the threshold. Your life's about to change! After this you'll never be the same."

"All this from soup?"

Her eyes sparkle. "Who's talkin' about soup?"

Slowly, and with a hint of sadness even I can detect in my voice, I confess: "I'm not very good at relationships, Trudy."

"Of course you are!"

I smile. "If you knew my history you wouldn't say that."

"Have you ever been in a healthy relationship?"

I think about it a minute, then say, "I think so. Once."

"And were you ready for it?"

"No."

"Then it don't count. Relationships are like opportunities. You have to be ready when they come. Are you at a place in your life where you're ready to begin a healthy relationship?"

I search her eyes. "I don't know. Maybe. I mean, I'd like to."

"You should start slowly and work your way up."

"That would suit me."

"Good. We'll start with parsley and cabbage."

"And after that?"

"The sky's the limit."

I say, "Make a list. I'll make sure you get everything you need."

She arches an eyebrow theatrically and says, "Don't be angry if I limit that list to soup ingredients. At least for the time bein'."

"Trudy?"

"Yes sir?"

"I'm glad you're here."

"Me too."

Bonus Scene #3: I Am the Cosmos

Trudy & Creed, POV: Third Person

TRUDY COOKING IN Creed's kitchen, hears music playing, follows the source to the den. Enters, says, "Such a sad song!"

He looks up. "Go ahead. Make fun of it."

She looks shocked. "Why would I do that?"

He sighs. "You're young. Times change. Music changes." He frowns. "You probably like the type of songs that—"

She holds up her hand. "I'll stop you now, before you presume to tell me what type of music I like. All you need to know about me is I could never make fun of a person who's in pain."

He studies her a moment. "You understand the words?"

She shakes her head. "No. The singer's too upset, and the arrangement's drownin' out his sorrowful voice. But I've known hard times and know a sad song when I hear it."

Creed nods. "The singer's saying, 'Every night I tell myself I am the cosmos, I am the wind. But that don't get you back again.'"

She stands there a moment, listening. Then says, "And this part is him sayin' over and over he really wants to see her again?"

Creed nods again, but there's a deep sadness in it. Trudy understands the connection: Creed would like to see his daughter again.

Trudy says, "Would you play it for me from the start?"

"Seriously?"

"Please?"

He replays the song and studies her face as she listens. When it's finished she looks at him and says, "I like it. It's about losin' someone you love."

"You don't think it's maudlin?"

"I don't know that word. But a song like that belongs in the universe, and should never be forgotten."

"Well said, Trudy."

"Thank you. It's just that...." She pauses.

"Go ahead."

"You played it three times straight before I came in."

"So?"

"There's a time and place for sad songs."

"And?"

"This might be the place, but it ain't the time."

"Why not?"

She smiles brightly. "Because I'm still *here*, of course!"

He looks at her and laughs.

She says, "But I'll warn you right now: if I ever leave, you're gonna wear that song out!"

He smiles. "So it's all about *you*, is it?"

"Nope." She grins and says, " But it *could* be."

"Why Trudy Lake!" he said.

"What?"

"Are you flirting with me?"

"Not yet."

"Will you tell me if you start?"

She smiles. "How about I tell you *when* I start!"

He smiles again. "Can I ask you just one question?"

"Is it rude?"

"It's not intended to be."

"Okay then."

He says, "Have you ever been with a woman?"

She starts to say something, then stops herself and cocks her head. "In what way?"

"Have you ever made love to a woman?"

She frowns. "No I have not." She pauses; then says, "Have *you*?"

He chuckles.

She turns to leave the room, then spins back around and says, "That was a really personal question, by the way. I barely know you."

"Sorry."

"It *was* rude."

"I suppose it seems that way, but I had a reason for asking. You see, in my last relationship—"

She holds her hand up again. "Don't do that. Don't compare me to someone else, 'cause first of all, your last relationship is personal to the two of you. And second, you and I aren't in a relationship."

"You're right of course. Except that a moment ago you said it's not about you, but it *could* be. I just thought maybe you were opening the door."

She tosses her hair. "An open door ain't the same as an invitation to enter."

He stares at her like she's one of those wooden Chinese puzzles that are easy to take apart but almost impossible to put back together. Then says, "Is that what we're doing? Gazing at each other through an open door?"

"I can't answer that till I know what door you're tryin' to open."

"You have a unique way of phrasing things."

"Thank you. By the way, your soup's ready."

THE END (For Real!)

Personal Message from John Locke:

If you like my books, you'll LOVE my mailing list! By joining, you'll receive discounts of up to 67% on future eBooks. Plus, you'll be eligible for amazing contests, drawings, and you'll receive immediate notice when my newest books become available!

Let the fun begin here:
http://www.donovancreed.com/Contact.aspx

Or visit my website, http://www.DonovanCreed.com

John Locke

New York Times Best Selling Author
8th Member of the Kindle Million Sales Club
(which includes James Patterson, Stieg Larsson, George R.R. Martin and Lee Child, among others)

John Locke had 4 of the top 10 eBooks on Amazon/Kindle at the same time, including #1 and #2!

...Had 6 of the top 20, and 8 books in the top 43 at the same time!

...Has written 25 books in four years in six separate genres, all best-sellers!

...Has been published in numerous languages by many of the world's most prestigious publishing houses!